Abington Square

Life is About Faith and Going into the Unknown

Cristina Guarneri

Chapter One

AISLING

Aisling Turnberry was just seventeen years old when she realized that she was different from her friend Maren. Aisling had a natural ability to create with special herbs and spices that her grandmother would give her. She knew that there was something magical about her life. Every Saturday morning, she and her grandmother Sara would walk up the steep rocks of their background and through the forest to Seeth Chapel.

"Come Aisling, let me show you what you need to know most to survive in this world," Sara told her granddaughter.

"What more would I need outside of education?" Aisling questioned.

"When I was about your age, I trusted people in the world," Sara confessed.

"What's wrong with trusting people, grandma?" Aisling asked.

"There isn't anything wrong with trusting people if they are the right people. When your mother and I first moved to Maple Hill, neighbors became suspicious of us because of my ability to heal people. They called us evil witches," she explained.

"Why would they believe that you were evil?" Aisling asked with confusion.

"Because I am a witch, you are a witch. Our whole family are witches, Aisling. That's why I say to trust a human would be a sin! Do you understand?" Sara asked.

"I understand, but I don't agree with you. Not everyone dislikes witches."

"My dear, one day you will when you least expect it. When you trust someone with all your heart, just like I did. Spare yourself the pain," Sara told her. "I'm going to take these three blue candles, three drops of clove oil, and one envelope, now you try," she watched, as Aisling did the same.

"Very good, my dear. Now take the blue ink, three pieces of paper, the Jasmine Oil, and put them into this fireproof bowl."

"Now write the names of those you want this spell to work on, and light the candles, too," Sara directed Aisling.

Aisling found comfort walking through the dark green trees that were in the back of their old Victorian home. It was the one place that she felt safest besides Seeth Chapel. Every witch needed a place to practice their spells and potions, as the chapel was where Sara would meet with Aisling and the other women of witchcraft. During the hours they spent together, locked within the mysteries of the forest. Each of the witches practiced peppermint potions and dried flower mixtures of spices. They were strong enough to put any person under a spell. Aisling watched as her grandmother would teach each woman a new potion.

"My dear, come join us here?" As Sara gathered her materials.

"No, I'd rather watch this time," Aisling told her.

Inside, Aisling had no desire to learn potions or to mix spices. Instead, she wanted to be like the other kids in her graduating class. She wanted to be human.

*****

By the time June came, Aisling and her one friend Maren Cornwall were ready to go to college. Maren was quiet and didn't have many friends by choice. She wanted to become just like the other women in her family, as she planned on becoming a midwife like her mother and her grandmother. Aisling, on the other hand, wanted to experience life. She had been accepted to four colleges and chose Sage University, forty miles north of Maple Hill. She hoped the time away from her grandmother would give her the chance to be like everyone else. The only problem was that she didn't tell Sara of her plans to attend Sage University.

*****

On a hot summer afternoon, Aisling and Maren had walked into their graduation ceremony carrying the same ruby red roses that her mother carried at her high school graduation. She wanted to make it a family tradition. Aisling's mother had died during childbirth and she never had the chance to meet her mother. Sara was the closest that she had to a mother, but even Aisling felt that as overbearing as her grandmother was, she had no one else.

Aisling listened to the music as it faded into the background. Her eyes were fixated on the audience, as she looked at the crowds of parents and grandparents that watched the procession of graduates.

"I wish my grandmother would have attended," Aisling whispered to Maren, as her eyes began to fill with tears.

"You never know, one day your grandmother just might change her mind about humans being a bad influence on witches and come to her senses," Maren assured her before giving her friend a quick embrace as they sat down in their seats.

"Imagine, on a special day like my graduation, Sara refuses to attend because it would mean that she would have to share the company of others who weren't witches," explained Aisling, as sarcasm filled her voice.

"A witch hunt of some sort, where all the bad witches hide from mortals out of fear of being hung. Besides, not all humans are hunting witches. Some of us like the chance of making a magic potion once in a while," Maren laughed out loud and flashed Aisling a smile.

The excitement of receiving her diploma made her feel like she could do anything. Walking the five blocks from school, Aisling found herself back home. Stopping to admire the house, she loved the old pink Victorian house that Sara had bought twenty years ago. Aisling loved how the house was accented with delicate red roses and white daisies.

Taking a seat on the pristine white swing that fashioned their front porch, she took a seat and listened to the chirping of the bluebirds.

As she opened the screen door, "I didn't hear you come in," said Sara, "how was the ceremony?" Sara stepped out onto the front porch and took a seat next to her granddaughter.

"It was beautiful, but it's just too bad you couldn't attend," Aisling told her. "We have been through this a hundred times. I will not go where there are humans," Sara answered sternly.

"Why not, they are people just like us," Aisling snapped.

"We are not like them. We are witches, and witches do not go where humans would be!"

"You are ridiculous!"

"Don't take that tone with me. You are one of us. You will take your place as a witch with me at Seeth Chapel."

"I don't see the point. I have no desire to be a witch. I've decided instead to go to college."

"College, since when did you decide that you would go to school?"

"When I received a full scholarship to Sage University."

"Sage University, that isn't a school for witches."

"No, it isn't."

"A regular college? You will do no such thing!"

"I want to be like others my age. Why can't you understand that?"

"Alright, then you will go to Zildabranch as I did, and like your mother, then you will join me at Seeth Chapel teaching the other witches."

"I won't go!"

"You will do as I say! *To trust a human would be a sin!*" Sara answered as Aisling stormed off into the house, before slamming the screen door.

"Aisling, you come back here!"

Stomping her feet up the stairs to her bedroom, Aisling stared outside the window and watched as her grandmother brought out a big black pot. She listened to Sara's words, *"to trust a human would be a sin!"* as the pot began to boil.

"I want no part of this life grandmother. I want no part of being a witch. I wish that my mother was alive. Then maybe I could go to college and be like humans," Aisling thought to herself, as she looked out the window.

A soft voice came from behind her, "Aisling," as she turned her head, a young woman with porcelain skin and flowing ginger hair stood before her. She dressed in all black; her eyes sparkled a deep blue.

"Who are you?" asked Aisling.

"It's me, your mother." Her long hair glistened. Outside of a few pictures when she was a baby, Aisling never met her mother, Cressida. After Aisling was born, she passed away due to complications from giving birth.

"You must listen to your grandmother. I know it's not what you want to do in life, but it's what's best for you. We can't trust this world. Remember, we are witches. Humans see witches as evil. Your grandmother is right when she says, *"to trust a human would be a sin!"*

"I don't want to be a witch. I want to go to college."

"Listen to your grandmother for me," Cressida told her as slowly disappeared, as she ran toward the vanishing ghost. Her eyes swelled with tears, if only she could have more time with her mother then maybe she would understand why it was so important for Aisling to be a witch.

Staring out her bedroom window, she began to cry as Sara continued to stir the big black pot. Turning away from the window, Aisling crawled into bed and under the sheets. She closed her eyes, the sky became a dark gray, and the roar of wind began to settle in, as the soft lilac curtains swayed in front of the open window, as a streak of lightning crossed the gray sky. She could hear her grandmother's words being repeated in her head, as the strength of wind picked up speed, *"To trust a human would be a sin!"*

Chapter Two

SARA

A strong wind overpowered the pale moonlit sky. For as long as she could remember, Sara had spent her life following the evil that so many people in the world were afraid of encountering, they feared witches, as they began to plague people everywhere. She opened the pages of an old tattered book that she had put together called Taika, her magic book. She didn't want any of her magic to be lost after she died. Sara was old, but she had spunk and she didn't look her age. She often wore black clothing and her dark brown hair came to her waist. No one would ever know that she had surpassed being one hundred years old. At the same time, she felt her body slipping. Nodding on and off into the darkness of her thoughts, she knew there wouldn't be much time left before passing away, as she thought back on her life.

Sara was born into a family of witches. At just thirty years old, Sara felt the pain and grief of losing her daughter, Cressida. Sara vowed to raise her granddaughter just as she did her daughter, but Aisling was nothing like her mother. Cressida believed in the power of witchcraft. Aisling had little interest in potions or learning spells. Sara had no other choice but to bring Aisling to attend Seeth Church. It was there that Aisling observed how destructive witchcraft could be, and she wanted no part of it. That was why it was easy to fall in love with someone like Miles

Dowse, a Christian man she would meet after bumping into him at the post office.

"Excuse me, is this yours?" handing Aisling the pink envelope that dropped from her hand.

"Thank you."

"You're welcome," he paused, as he smiled at her. "I'm Miles."

"Aisling," she answered with a smile.

"Next!" announced the postal worker. Startled by his voice, she dropped the envelope next to Miles' feet. Picking up the envelope, he watched Aisling fumble through her letters.

"I'd like to mail these."

"That will be four dollars and fifty cents."

"Fifty cents change," as Miles slipped the fallen envelope to her, she turned around to answer him.

"Oh, thank you. I must have dropped this," she said, as she looked at the pink envelope. On it he wrote a message: Call me, Miles Dowse. Aisling was surprised to read his message. She would never think to call a guy before, but maybe this time it would be different.

"Thanks, I will," as they walked out of the post office together.

Aisling hid Miles' phone number in her pocket so that Sara wouldn't see it.

"Should I call," picking up the phone and then hanging up, "maybe it could wait just one more day," she thought to herself.

"Remember, to trust a human would be a sin!" Aisling could hear her grandmother's voice in her head. "Shut up," she whispered to herself, as she stuffed the folded the envelope with Mile's phone number into her pocket.

"Grandma! I'm going to the market!" she yelled, but Sara didn't answer. Aisling assumed her grandmother was at Seeth Chapel. She opened the worn screen door and walked down the steps toward Sterling Markets.

Aisling often enjoyed walking down the tree-lined streets of Maple Hill. There were always new experiences of seeing people she had never seen before. Fiddling with her pants pocket, the envelope with Miles' number fell out of her jeans. Bending over to pick it up, a pair of brown Dockers starred at her. Looking up, she was taken aback by what she saw, it was Miles.

"I know you," he joked. "You're the girl from the post office," flashing a smile at her.

"And you're Miles, right?"

"Well, at least you didn't forget my name." He gave a smile.

"I was meaning to call you, but —" Aisling confessed.

"But you lost my number," he joked, as he gave her back the envelope.

"No, it's complicated."

"Another man?"

"No, nothing like that. It's just that I'm kind of kept under lock and key, and you're a human."

"I'm human? I don't know what that means. Aren't you?" Miles joked.

"Well, yeah," Aisling gave way to an uncomfortable laugh. "I'm a human, but I'm different than you are."

"Why, because you're a girl?" Miles further joked.

"No, it's a long story," Aisling gave Miles a slight punch to his left arm.

"Look, since you never called me. Why don't we make a plan to see each other this weekend?" Miles asked.

"Well...I don't know," Aisling hesitated, as she looked away from him, as a women was selling yellow, white, red, and pink roses from her stand nearby. Miles walked over and a bought a bouquet of lavender roses.

"This is the second time in weeks we've run into each. I won't take no for an answer," he said as he handed Aisling the flowers.

"I know we've just met, and I don't know what my feelings are yet, but I sure do like you enough to give you roses," Miles smiled.

"Okay, you've convinced me," she said with a smile.

"Good, you won't regret it."

Holding the beautifully colored lavender flowers, all that Aisling could think about was her grandmother's reaction to dating a human. *"To trust a human would be a sin!"*

"Okay," answered Aisling.

"Where do you live?"

"Where?" she thought about Sara's reaction.

"Yeah, where?"

"427 Acorn Drive," the words came out of her mouth before thinking.

"I'll pick you up at 7 then," Miles confirmed with a bright smile.

"Okay, see you then," Aisling answered before parting ways.

*****

After three days of waiting anxiously for Saturday to arrive, Aisling felt the pain of pins and needles throughout her body. How was she going to explain to Sara about Miles? She put on the finishing touches on her makeup and walked out of the bathroom.

"Where are you going?" Sara asked suspiciously.

"Out— with a friend," Aisling said under her breathe.

"A friend— do you mean Maven from high school?"

"No grandma, someone new. His name is Miles," Aisling answered.

"Miles, who is he?" asked Sara curiously.

"Someone I met at the post office," Aisling said non-chalantly.

"Is he like us, a witch?" asked Sara.

"No, he's not," Aisling spoke with a nervous tone.

"Then he's a human!" Sara's voice raised. "What have I said to you all along, *to trust a human would be a sin!*" Sara's words echoed as the doorbell rang.

"I got to go," Aisling said, brushing off Sara's words.

From behind the kitchen, Sara took a look at Miles tall height and dark hair from the door.

"Are you ready?" Miles asked.

"Yeah, bye Grandmother," as she waved goodbye.

Taking the big black pot out of the cabinet, Sara began to pour licorice and sage together. "Tousles, stoles, and drops. I must begin to change his heart." It was her favorite spell for getting rid of people. It angered Sara and the last thing that she wanted was a man influencing her granddaughter.

The dark brown walls were worn, as they held the secret potions and spells of the Taika. For hours, Sara pulled bottles of cinnamon, dandelion, and cat's claw off of the wooden shelf that sat fashionably against the sturdiness of the dimly lit room. Each mixture that she made was poured into empty crystal bottles. Sara would wait for Miles at the front door for him to sprinkle him with one of her spells.

"Hello, you must be Aisling's grandmother," Miles put his hand out to Sara.

"I am," Sara said sternly, as she sprinkled a mixture of spices on him.

"Why are you here?" Sara's tone was serious and stern.

"I'm here to pick up Aisling. Is she ready?" Miles asked.

"She's not here!"

"Grandmother! I'm right here," Aisling corrected.

"For a minute there I thought you might have forgotten," Miles gave a half smile.

"My grandmother likes to be funny," Aisling explained, taking her coat to walk out the door.

"Nonsense, I never joke. To trust a human would be a sin!" Sara warned as she pinched Aisling's arm.

"Are you ready to go," Aisling quickly took Miles's hand and walked down the steps.

Sara's eyes followed her granddaughter's move, as they walked toward town. She had made up her mind that no man would get in the way of her granddaughter. Aisling would be a witch no matter what the cost. Aisling would keep to the traditions that she learned.

"Here," Miles had given Aisling a bouquet of red roses.

"Roses— they're beautiful."

"Roses are an expression of love," Miles confessed.

"That's pretty deep for a first date don't you think?" Aisling joked as she smelled the sweet aroma of the flowers. Truth is, she never had gotten flowers before from anyone, and it was a beautiful gesture.

"Maybe, but you never know what tomorrow will bring, you know. One minute we're here and the next we're gone," Miles told her.

"I guess so," Aisling answered.

"Anyway, flowers are my way of talking."

"What do you mean? You have a voice, Miles. Why do you need flowers to speak for you?"

"They don't speak for me, they send a message."

"Couldn't you just say it? Why do you give lavender flowers?" Aisling questioned. "Why not red ones?"

"It's like this," taking a rose from Aisling's bouquet. "Take this rose, it's an unmistakable expression of love," Miles handed her back the rose.

"So this rose means love, okay," Aisling wasn't convinced in what Miles was saying.

"You don't believe me?"

"No," Aisling answered.

"Okay, how bout this. The Lily is for beauty, carnations are for innocence."

"I love carnations," Aisling added.

"Good to know, but pay attention. The Iris is for eloquence, And the Daisy—."

"Okay, I get it, but you don't have to give me a lesson on every flower," Aisling said with a smile.

"Lavender roses means love at first sight," Miles spoke softly. Aisling felt her face become flush. She couldn't help but fear what kind of spell that her grandmother would put on Miles. She could hear Sara's words in her head, *to trust a human would be a sin!*" Aisling quickly shook her head to get her grandmother's voice out of her head, as dinner was brought over of savory potatoes and oven-roasted chicken and some chocolate thing that Aisling couldn't stop eating.

After dinner, Miles and Aisling took a stroll outside of the restaurant. The bushes of roses showed brightly under the string of small twinkle lights that decorated the outside area of the restaurant.

"This was great!" She looked down at the fragrant roses. "I had a good time." Aisling turned her eyes toward Miles.

"I'm glad, it was gorgeous night out," Miles starred up at the clouds in the dark blue sky, as silence filled the town streets, while a crowd inside the restaurant was busy chatting and eating.

"It's been a perfect night, Aisling," Miles didn't know what else to say.

"I agree," as Aisling fiddled with her hands.

"I guess I should take you home early," Miles told her.

"What for, it's pretty early."

"It is, but I want to get on your grandmother's good side. If I keep you out late, she may never let me see you again," he explained.

"Good thinking, Miles," she smiled. "I was getting nervous about the time and my grandmother's reaction to my being out late."

"It's only 9:30 and the night still has a ton of hours left in it."

"For you, Miles. But my grandmother wouldn't understand. I shouldn't even be out. I should be home helping her," Aisling became quiet.

"Well I don't know anything about your grandmother, but you're a young girl. You should be out and doing things," Miles flashed her a smile.

"You're very nice, Miles. But I'm not sure where this could go," she explained.

"Where what could go? I don't get it— we're two adults, Aisling."

"It's so much more complicated than us being adults, Miles," she looked down on gold link watch. "I should go, it's getting late. Thank you for a great time," Aisling said before leaving. Miles watched as she disappeared into the dark midnight air. Not a trace of her could be found anywhere.

*****

The next morning, the doorbell rang at the early hour of eight o'clock.

"Who's visiting at this time," Sara scolded.

"Delivery!" yelled a young man's voice. Sara opened the door to a large bouquet of tulips.

"I didn't order anything," questioned Sara in a serious tone.

"They're for Aisling Turnbery, ma'am. Is that you?" asked the delivery boy.

"I'm her grandmother," she said while signing the delivery receipt and closing the door behind her.

"Who is grandma?" Aisling came down from her bedroom in her nightgown.

"These are for you," directed Sara sternly, "Probably from that boy you saw last night." Sara put the flowers down on a wooden table next to the living room. Aisling took the card that was signed by Miles and gave a wide smile.

Every Saturday, at eight o'clock, like clockwork, the doorbell would ring and Aisling received a bouquet of lavender roses.

"I don't like it, Aisling. And I don't like him!"

"You don't even know him, grandma, but he's a nice person."

"He's a human and as long as he's not a witch, he will never be a nice person to me. He will never be good enough for you," Sara scowled.

*****

With all of her might, Sara tried every potion she could think of from her book, but it wasn't enough, as she began to spend more time at Seeth Chapel creating new ones. But soon, Aisling and Miles had been dating for six months and then eight months.

"Grandmother, where are you!" Aisling yelled, she saw Sara walk into the forest. Walking the path to Seeth Chapel, she could hear Sara's voice. Thunder began to rumble in the sky, even though it was still a clear blue color.

"I'm in here, Aisling," as she entered the church doors.

"Grandmother, what are you doing?"

"Making a new batch of potions," she answered. "Come and help."

"No, grandmother, I don't want to help. I want to spend some time with Miles."

"Nonsense, he has too great a faith. You are a witch, you're not human. To trust a human would be a sin, Aisling!"

"What if I don't want to be a witch?" Aisling questioned.

"You have no choice. This is the life that you are given, Aisling" as Sara put together a batch of cat's claw and sage together.

"This will keep Miles away for good," Sara thought to herself.

Taking a big black pot into the backyard, Sara began to put together a harsh and strong aroma of Jasmine and Carrion. "Tousles, stoles, and drops. I must begin to change his heart." It was then that her energies were released. Smoke steamed from the heavy boiling pot. The smells were inviting to Sara, as she took in a deep breath. "Tousles, stoles, and drops. I must begin to change his heart," she repeated until the roar of thunder echoed in the sky, as a heavy wind and a downpour of rain came storming down on her. Wrapped in full black clothing, she stirred and stirred as hard as she could. It was more than any woman her age should be doing. She was desperate, and she would do anything to get rid of Miles. Sara was getting older, and it wouldn't be long when the time would come when she would pass away.

"Tousles, stoles, and drops. I must begin to change his heart," Sara repeated.

The rains became heavier and heavier, to the point of torrential rain, as the floodwaters overcame the area. Tousles, stoles, and drops. I must begin to change his heart. Aisling paid no mind to Sara. It wasn't the first time that she had cooked up a spell. She was pleased to have finished her studies in healing. The future was bright for her, at least that's what she thought. Miles had never told her his true plans for his life had nothing to do with her. It wasn't that he didn't care for it, but his faith was the one driving force that kept him out of trouble and onto the path of righteousness.

Chapter Three

MILES

Miles turned to the church even as a young child. Having faith was more important to him than a relationship, but he knew that his words struck Aisling hard, especially the first time that he realized that they were becoming a couple. "I hear nothing but the sound of my heart beating when it's you that takes my breath away. Not even the sound of a sweet lullaby or the softness of a rose petal could take my breath away as easily as your presence," he told her on their six-month anniversary.

Her face glowed brightly at his words. But even with such strong feelings, being a clergyman meant that marriage would never be in the cards for him. And Miles was certainly not in any position to provide for himself, let alone a wife and a child, at least not on what little he would be making as part of the church. He would embarrass himself what kind of man is unable to provide for himself or even a family. Besides, Miles saw that Aisling had ambition and drive since he was just the opposite growing up. His parents were relieved to hear that he decided to enter ministry and become a part of the clergy.

Miles always felt like a disappointment. He didn't go to Vanderbilt like his brother, Cole. He never wanted to become a rich businessman or doctor like his brother. Cole, unlike Miles, was well-mannered, a Wall Street Broker who grew up reading books and watching old movies. Cole was the quiet one of the family. Miles was no saint growing up. He hung around with the wrong crowd and got himself into trouble more times than he could count on two hands, drinking and breaking into car windows. It wasn't something that he was proud of, but he took those experiences with him as he thought about becoming a part of the clergy after Father Welk caught Miles stealing money out of the church offering.

"I see you, Miles Downing!" he scolded, as Miles hid in a side pew.

"I see the money in your hands! As Miles dropped it on the shiny tilled floor.

"I'm sorry, Father. It's that my family has little money for food." A lie, Miles wouldn't tell the truth. Besides, alcohol was more important to him than his relationship with a priest.

"If it's food that you need, we can help you. But let's not forget that there is something more than physical food that you need."

"What do you mean?"

"Spiritual food that our bodies need, Miles" he reminded, "There's a great plan for your life if you'd just believe."

He would never forget Father Welk and the great plan that he believed was in store for Miles. Easily, he could have been arrested for stealing, but when he wasn't, Miles took it as getting his second chance to start anew, to make up for all the mistakes that he made in his life.

Thinking back on the time that he spent with Aisling, Miles couldn't help but remember when he heard that Aisling was pregnant. He wasn't prepared to become a father. Instead, Miles was prepared to tell her of his plans of leaving for seminary school.

"I can't get the sound of Aisling's tears out of my head," he told himself, as he packed the last of his belongings.

Taking a picture off of the dark oak bedroom mirror of Aisling and him sitting on the front steps, he stared at the picture and thought about how much he would miss her. They looked so happy and carefree. It didn't feel the same anymore. His life and priorities have changed since deciding to enter seminary school. Miles stared closely at the picture, the alarm of his watch signaled it was time to go, as he picked up his bags and walked out the front door of the modest two-family home of red brick and white shingles that he was renting, as Miles thought about how different it would be living somewhere else. Taking one last look at the house, he walked the short two blocks to the train station; he stood impatiently at the platform.

Miles got on the eight o'clock train to set out for seminary. He thought about calling Aisling but resisted the urge as he settled into his seat and looked out the window. Passengers filled the waiting area of the platform. Miles watched the people get on the long line in front of the booking window. Everyone seemed to be in a hurry, as passengers were waiting eagerly to get on the train. Some were sitting on benches and smoking or reading newspapers. A few were waving good-bye to passengers seated on the train.

There was commotion everywhere, and a great rush at the doors of compartments, as passengers got to their seats, as the whole platform was full of noise before passengers had settled.

"All Aboard!" Yelled the conductor. The final call to depart hit Miles hard, as he felt sadness and wondered if he was making a mistake leaving Aisling behind. The train's engine whistled, as it began to move. There was waving of hands and handkerchiefs, as the train gained speed. Miles looked at the platform. It looked like a deserted place once again. He closed his eyes to the soft sound of the train.

It would take hours before reaching Trinity Seminary.

"Last Stop, Abington Square!"

Miles opened his eyes to see the lush green grass and tall oak trees that lined the main street. Abington Square would now become his home. Aisling was far away from him by hours and by spirit. Taking his bags out from the dark gray overhead compartment, Miles walked down the steps off the train and hailed a taxi to school.

"Where to?" Asked a man in his mid-fifties. Miles looked around at his surroundings.

"I said, where to?" the driver asked again.

"Oh, sorry. Trinity Seminary," Miles responded, as he put his bags in the backseat next to him and closed the door.

Taking the drive up the winding road that was lined by the fragrant evergreen trees, he listened to the trickling raindrops that began to hit the taxi window.

"We've been getting a lot of rain this time of year. Are you a new student?" asked the taxi driver.

"I'm a student. How did you know?" asked Miles.

"I could tell. You all act the same, quiet and overwhelmed by the scenery," said the taxi driver.

"It is beautiful here. I've never seen trees like this before."

"Where are you from that you haven't seen evergreen trees?" asked the taxi driver.

"It's not that I haven't seen evergreens before, but never this green."

"It's what makes Abington Square a great place to live. The seminary has the most evergreen trees in town. I think the school likes it that way so that it keeps the campus closed off from the visitors that come to Abington Square," informed the taxi driver. "I'm guessing since you're attending Trinity that you will become a priest."

"I am, I want to help the poor," answered Miles, as they came up given a dark brownstone building. Its arched-shaped windows gave its exterior character. The grounds looked freshly mowed and decorated with dark green bushes and a stream of pure white water. Miles was taken back by the beauty of Trinity, as the taxi stopped in front of the tall maple doors.

"That'll be ten dollars," said the taxi driver, as Miles paid him. "Good luck to you," the taxi driver said.

"Thanks, man," as he paid the driver.

"Maybe I'll see you in town. Make sure to see Paige Chapel. It's just as beautiful as this campus," the taxi driver offered.

"I will," said Miles as he opened the door and took his bags out before entering the front door and into the quietness of Trinity Seminary.

Over the next month, and the months after that, Miles focused on nothing but his studies. From time to time, he thought about Aisling and her life. Once in a while he thought about the baby and if it was even born yet. It wasn't that he didn't care, but rather, he wouldn't let anything stand in the way of his commitment to the church.

Taking out a piece of plain white paper, he began to write a letter to Aisling. As he began to write, he wasn't sure anymore what to say.

Dear Aisling: My day starts at 5 am when the alarm goes off, this is my goal, though I'm not always successful: the race to turn in assignments on time sometimes leads to late nights and later mornings. This morning, though, is a good one – I'm up on time and start the coffee brewing. Even though I'm a morning person, I still find it hard to get up most mornings. Coffee helps, and so does my Bible study. Since I enjoy it, it makes for motivation to get up and have some quiet, relaxed, unhurried time – a rare commodity in my day! Today, I'm studying in 2 Peter and making some notes in this booklet about what I have learned. I am trying to get into the habit of taking a walk around my neighborhood. Today is a good day, though much of this spring has been unseasonably wet and rainy. I go down to the seminary kitchen, where the other students and I make some breakfast: sometimes eggs, and even some peanut butter oatmeal, and milk.

I often have class in the afternoon, so I spend most of my time studying in the morning or going for long walks. I often think about you. This morning though I focused on writing a paper on 2 Peter, and preparing for a class that I will be involved in at my church. When I graduate, I will work at Paige Chapel not far from campus. It's beautiful here. I think that you would like it. The beautiful Evergreen trees will take your breath away. Sometimes I take a break to play my cello – a hobby that often falls to the wayside when I feel overloaded on assignments. I still don't sound that great when presenting sermons, but I'm trying hard. I try to take advantage of the time by listening to books to help me when speaking. The seminary often hosts informational lunches to acquaint students with different ministries. Today they have a meeting about Reaching and Teaching, a missions organization that I appreciate. It was great to hear from these guys over lunch.

After lunch, I spend some time studying in the library, this is one of the highlights of attending Trinity, and there is no place that is more epic to study in than this! Because I live a little ways from school, I try to group my classes into a couple of days each week. I have six hours of lecture with an hour break in the middle. Today includes both New Testament and Old Testament Survey. It's me, trying to make it through the last few hours of class. The content is great, but it is a lot of time to be sitting. When I finally get back to my room, it is past 10 pm. It's time to end the day, like the campus, and the floor that I live on is already dark and quiet inside. You should visit. Abington Square is beautiful. ~ Miles

Taking the letter, he sealed it tightly shut and sent it with a bouquet of blue Irises to symbolize hope. Miles only hoped that she would get it and that her grandmother wouldn't open it up and shred it. Miles knew that Sara didn't like him because he was human. He placed a stamp on the envelope and put it in the mail. Three, maybe four days, Aisling would get his letter. Maybe she would be intrigued to visit Trinity. Maybe she would leave her grandmother's house and move to Abington Square. Then Miles could get away from the guilt for not being there for the baby.

To Miles, joining the church was his way to find forgiveness. He spent years feeling guilty for not being a part of Sloane's life growing up. "Move to Abington Square, Aisling so that I can guide Sloane," he begged her, so to make it up to her. If he couldn't be the father he hoped to be for her, at the very least, he could be there for her with spiritual guidance.

AISLING

It took five days for Aisling to get the letter that Miles had written her, but she never opened it. Her contractions were becoming stronger and more frequent. She took the letter and hid it between her mattress and box spring so that Sara wouldn't find it. She thought about the last time that she saw Miles and their conversation outside of her house.

"Aisling, you know that I want to be here with you and the baby," Miles told her.

"I think we can be a happy family, Miles."

"Your grandmother hates me too much, I'm human, and I'm a Christian."

"She doesn't trust humans. Remember, she believes in a different way of life. Different than my way. I come from a long line of witchcraft," Aisling explained.

"You see, that's a problem for me, Aisling."

"I know it is, but I do believe in a higher power," Aisling tried to convince him.

"You say that and I believe it, but do you believe in God? Do you believe he died for you?" Aisling stood silent as she stared deeply into Miles' eyes.

"Of course I do," she answered.

"That's important, you know because I believe my calling is to serve God," Miles stressed.

"What do you mean?" she asked.

"I mean, there is never going to be the right time to say this," he told her.

"What, what is it?"

"I'm leaving. I'm going into the seminary in a few days," Miles could see the confusion in her deep blue eyes.

"For how long?" She asked.

"As long as it takes, Aisling. Ministry is my life."

"What about the baby, what about us?"

"My faith and service to ministry have to come first, you understand," Miles explained.

"So you're leaving just like that?" She asked as her grandmother appeared at the door.

"I have to go Aisling," Miles said as he walked away from her.

"I think we could be good together," Aisling begged.

"I have to go. I leave for seminary soon, and it's my choice, the reason why I am on this Earth," Miles explained.

"When were you going to tell me that you were leaving?" Asked Aisling. Miles could see the shadow of Sara's frame in the doorway.

"I got to go," Miles told her as she turned to walk away. He could see her Aisling sobbing, but he refused to look back at her. He knew if he looked at her, he might not ever fulfill his destiny of being in the church.

Besides, it was better this way. Aisling would be cared for by her grandmother, who was committed to being a witch. Walking up the steps of the front porch, Sara came from behind the door.

"I told you Aisling, never try a human. They will hurt you. They will break your heart," Sara warned her.

"Grandma he's different. He's not like the others."

"Yes, yes he is, Aisling. He was like your grandfather. He wasn't like us, and he left me alone too. Come, come with me and we make a new potion for your baby," Sara told her, as they walked inside the house. That was nine months ago. Standing in her bedroom, a strong jab of pain from a contraction.

"I got to throw up," Aisling yelled as Sara walked into her room. Her body was hot, heavy, and in pain. She felt like this nightmare would never end.

*****

It was as if she had gone to hell and back, though the fire continued to burn. Yes, this moment was supposed to be sweet and memorable, except it wasn't. Aisling wanted all the agonizing to end. Right here. Right now. She needed air. "Get this thing out of me!" she shouted, squeezing her grandmother's hand tightly, as she waited for the midwife to arrive. If the baby didn't leave her body soon, she might faint.

"You need water," Sara chanted, like Maven, Aisling's midwife came into the room.

"Is the position comfy enough for you?" Maven asked. "It's time to start pushing."

"Push," Maven told her, but nothing was happening. All Aisling wanted was for Maven to be quiet. "Shut up!!" she screamed, still heaving and pushing steadily. Sara went by the bed and held up one of her daughter's legs to help.

"Grandma," Aisling said, relieved to see her.

"Its fine, all you need to do is keep breathing." They went on like this for a while, as she breathed, chanted, and pushed. It was a repeated cycle. Aisling, feeling drowsy, was beginning to pass out. Who knew how long she had left to continue like this as Sara began to speak a spell of words.

*****

Aisling stayed in bed; the pain was clear on her face. She screamed every five seconds, hoping the baby would shoot out easily. Though, that wasn't the case. Aisling tried breathing excuses as the midwife suggested, yet, still, the contractions continued to wear her down, as a gush of water came out of her body.

"It's time," Maven told Sara. "Aisling, I'm going to need you to push."

"This isn't good," Maven exclaimed. She widened his eyes. "It looks like something isn't right with her. It's the umbilical cord; it's wrapped around her neck."

"What does that mean?!" Aisling yelled through her pushing and pain.

"If we don't get the baby out now, she is going to die," Maven told Sara.

"Do a C-section," Sara said.

"It's too late. By the time we get Aisling's medical attention, the baby will be dead. I'm sorry, but we're going to have to rely on our faith alone for this to happen," Maven told Aisling and Sara
Aisling listened as she pushed and pushed long and hard. An hour passed before they made progress. The head finally showed, "please come out baby, Aisling thought to herself, as the baby arrived.

"Aisling," Sara said, "What have you decided to name your daughter?"

Aisling sat up in her bed and nodded, saying, "Grandmother, I have decided on the name Sloane." Taking the baby in her arms, Sara rocked her back and forth.

"Remember my dear Sloane, to trust a human would be a sin." Aisling shook her head in disappointment as she said her grandmother's words, but at the same time, she was excited to start a new chapter in her life.

Chapter
Four

SARA

In less than a year after Sloane had been born, Sara became sicker. She was proud to be one of the first accused witches to have confessed that she in fact a witch working for the Devil. It's what sparked a massive witch hunt throughout Maple Hill when she was just a teenager. Sara remembered it vividly, like it was yesterday. She sat motionless in bed before turning her eyes toward Aisling, who was sitting next to her.

"My dear granddaughter remember everything that I have taught you. When I pass away, you must keep to my spells. You must keep the family tradition of witchcraft alive," Sara told her.

Aisling made no promises, as she watched her grandmother slowly pass away, but before her death, she had given the book of potions to Sloane. She told her the same words as she told Aisling throughout her childhood, *"To trust a human would be a sin. To trust in human power would be an even bigger sin. You have the power to overtake everyone. Use my book, and you will have anything that you want from this world."*

Aisling and Sloane had buried her next to Seeth Church. It's what she would have wanted. With no other choices left, she began to use honey and natural ingredients to help people, but the more she tried to help, the more suspicious they began to think of her as a witch. Aisling knew she needed a safe environment for Sloane. She took the sheets off of her bed. A thin white envelope fell out from between the mattress and box spring.

"What is this?" Aisling asked herself as she looked at the handwriting on the envelope.

"Miles, this is his handwriting." Aisling closed the door to her bedroom and found the letter that she never opened years ago. She read it line by line, savoring each word that he wrote. "When I graduate, I will be working in Paige Chapel. Come to visit. Abington Square is beautiful," she read. Aisling found her second chance in life. The chance to find faith and hope.
Aisling waited until Sloane was old enough to understand the stories of her grandmother Sara, Aisling decided to leave the life she knew behind for her daughter.

"Sloane, I've been waiting a long time for us to find a new home," Aisling told her.

"Where are we going, and why do we have to move?" Sloane asked.

"It's time to go on a new adventure. Someplace far away from here," Aisling tried with her all her might to make it sound exciting.

"I don't want to leave?" Sloane cried as she looked at the suitcases that were already packed.

"I know that it will be hard in the beginning, but you will make new friends, maybe even lifelong friends. We have to leave the grandmother's house behind. There are too many reminders of her here," Aisling confessed.

Taking their bags, Aisling and Sloane walked the few blocks to the train station. It was good to leave. Aisling could never understand why she was born a witch. More than ever, she wanted the faith that Miles had in his life. Maybe someday she would too, but not now when Sloane is older.

Then she would tell her daughter about Miles and why they moved to Abington Square.

ABINGTON SQUARE

The small town charm of Abington Square brought thousands of people to visit. What people loved most about the town was its gothic style buildings that gave it its charm and inspiration to writers from all over the world. Although the town's greatest appeal was its church, Paige Chapel. Inside it's sanctuary, visitors came just to see its soaring arches. Its mission was to bring people inside in hopes of finding faith, peace, inspiration, and courage.

As beautiful of a town as Abington Square was, it was also a place that was going through a dark time. More hundred people had begun to practice witchcraft. Father Miles Dowse knew witchcraft was a part of Abington Square. He became the senior clergyman of Paige Chapel. Tall, dark, and handsome, he was the most eligible bachelors in Abington Square. He paid no mind to that, as his pride and joy were in the Chapel. No one knew it better than he did, but outside of the luster of Paige Chapel, there was still a devout and strongly religious community that began to live in isolation because of their fear of the Devil and witches.

As Aisling and Sloane got off the one o'clock train, they felt so much hope for something better, as they walked into Fairchild's for lunch. Aisling and Sloane took a seat at a small table near the window. A young girl was sitting next to them.

"What are you reading?" Sloane asked the young girl.

"Some magazine that one of the nuns gave me?"

"Nuns?" asked Sloane.

"Yeah, I live at Paige Chapel. I help the nuns with their chores. My name is Abigail."

"Sloane, Sloane Turnberry."

"Do you work too? How old are you?" Abigail asked.

"I'm seventeen going on eighteen soon. I work with my mom. We are nurses," answered Sloane.

"Do you want to sit with us?" asked Aisling.

"You sure I wouldn't be a bother?"

"No, not at all," Aisling told her, as Abigail moved to their table.

"You said you live at Paige Chapel. Where is it?" Aisling asked, thinking about Miles.

"It's across the street. I live with two nuns and our clergyman, Father Miles," taking a bite from her sandwich.

"Is he married? I've never heard of a priest living with nuns," Aisling explained. In her heart, she knew it was Miles, her Miles.

"I don't think so. Father Mile seems uninterested in women."

"Why do you say that?" asked Sloane.

"Well once, our town doctor asked Father Miles about past his past relationships before entering the seminary. He was very distant and said very little about it, except that he had to choose between answering the call of God or marrying his girlfriend," Abigail told them.

Aisling's heart seemed to ache at Abigail's words, "a relationship that he hasn't gotten over," she only hoped that this someone was her. It's been years since she saw Miles. She felt guilty for never answering his letter before Sloane was born, but how could she. He left her brokenhearted. More importantly, he left his daughter.
The ring of the store door's bell brought a crowd of people in for Fairchild's lunch special of their moist turkey sandwiches filled with stuffing and warm bowls of creamy soup.

"Ching! Ching!" The bell seemed never to stop chiming, as Aisling, Sloane, and Abigail sat watching the people pass by. There were Dr. Matthews and the town's postman.

"Ching! Ching!"

"Father, good to see," said Dr. Matthews.

Aisling looked up from her sandwich to see the dark-haired man walking through the door. He looked just as she remembered him. Tall and lean, he still had that quiet way about him, as he shook Dr. Matthews' hand.

"That's Father Miles," Abigail told them, as Aisling's heart skipped a beat.

"Father!" yelled Abigail as she called him over.

"Abigail, I didn't know that you were here," said Miles as he walked over to their table.

"I want you to mean my new friend Sloane and her mom."

"Aisling," Miles interrupted. "How long have you been in town?"

"I just got here today," she told him.

"I'm glad you're here. I wondered if you ever got my letter."

"Letter?" answered Sloane.

"This is—?" Miles asked, pointing to Sloane.

"Sloane, my name is Sloane," she interrupted.

"That's a beautiful name," he said, as looked over at Aisling. Sloane had the same deep brown eyes and smile as Miles did. Just looking at her, he knew that was his daughter. The daughter that he hadn't seen in seventeen years.

"It's nice meeting you, Sloane."

"You too," she responded.

"Well, I better get back to Dr. Matthews. It was good seeing you, Aisling. Stop by the chapel when you get a chance. It would be good to catch up again," Miles offered before walking away.

"Come on, we've got to go," Aisling told her daughter, as she paid the check.

"Maybe I can stop by Paige Chapel," Sloane told Abigail.

"That would be great. I'm always around, usually with the nuns," as she waved goodbye to Aisling and Sloane.

"Ching! Ching!"

Miles watched as they walked out of the store and down the block until they were out of sight.

Chapter Five

ABIGAIL

Abigail Winslow never thought of herself as someone who lived in fear, but for the last two months, she found Sloane taunted herself. Sloane was her best friend, but she also came from a long line of women in her family who believed in the solemn powers of magic.

"I can feel the power of the sky changing from light to dark," Sloane told Abigail.

She didn't understand what made Sloane tell her such stories. Abigail knew that Sloane and her family were different from most in town, but she didn't believe that they could be full witches. Maybe a few magic spells, but nothing that would be too serious. Since moving to Abington Square, Abigail and Sloane were very close, as they went to church and studied together.

Sloane was the closest to the family as she would get. Abigail never met her parents. As a young child, she was adopted by the nuns of Paige Chapel. Even with her close ties to the church, many in town thought of them as inseparable, and they were right. With their long red hair and fair skin, their blues eyes would have easily mistaken them for twins. Maybe in many ways, they were like twins. They were the only two who knew each other's deepest secrets.

"You must swear not to tell a soul what my family and I are doing," Sloane warned her.

"I know that it is nothing," Abigail assured her, as the two promised a vow of protection to one another. Maybe, Sloane, had a few magic spells up her sleeve, it certainly didn't make her be a witch.

"I always enjoy coming to your house, Abigail. I wish that I knew the faith that you do," Sloane confessed.
Abigail wasn't sure how to witness to her. She too was learning more about faith, as she often listened to the nuns.

"So what if her family didn't believe in modem medicine. It wasn't so bad to practice a way of healing that brought the best out of people, and anyway, modern medicine isn't the most advanced. If it were, then so many people wouldn't be dying" Sloane thought to herself.

*****

Sloane knew that it was because of her mother and her grandmother who taught her everything that she knew on how to heal Scarlett Fever. Yet no matter how sick people became around her, Abigail wasn't able to get the answers she was looking for. When Sloane had learned how sick her friend was, it was Aisling that put together a mixture of licorice and other herbs together for healing. Abigail never quite understood it, but for a few words, and many sips of some honey-scented mixture. All that she knew was that she was healed. Since then, she never questioned Sloane or her family. Maybe she was afraid to ask, or maybe she was afraid to hear the truth, but in Abigail's mind, Sloane and her family were like any other person in Abington Square. *"Remember, you swore not to tell a soul,"* Sloane reminded her. *"We are soul sisters."*

AISLING

The slate tile eloquently laid on the kitchen floor of the old wooden home that sat close to the water and the Maple Hill Forest. A large porcelain pot sat on the large wood stove. Aisling couldn't shake off the feelings that she had about Miles since seeing him in Fairchild's. It was as if time had stopped, she too never married. After having Sloane, she held on to the thought that someday Miles would return to her. Instead, she found herself with a newborn baby and very little money. It was just Aisling and Sloane; they only had each other. She could never explain where her daughter's father was, that would be a story to be saved when Sloane got older. Telling her now would complicate everything. Aisling wasn't ready to open that chapter of her life up again. She was too busy building a life for them in Abington Square. *Someday I will tell, just not today,"* she reminded herself.

Over the years, Aisling turned to care for the sick. She often spent her time when she wasn't working singing songs, as a stew of oils and turmeric lavished the porcelain pot. Often used to heal, it was Aisling who was called to care for the sick in the town. Abington Square had very few nurses, but few truly believed in her witchery. She could never tell anyone why she and Sloane truly moved to Abington Square. After meeting Miles at Paige Chapel when Sloane had gone to bed late one night, she swore to Miles to not say a word. Only they would know the real reason that she and Sloane were in Abington Square.

"Aisling, you must not let on about Sloane and I.," he told her. "If anyone should find out that I am her father, I could lose everything. My parish, my position in Abington Square, everything."

"I promise, Miles. I won't tell a soul, but only on one condition, you must know your daughter, Sloane even if it means as a clergyman." "I will, Aisling," Miles confirmed.

"You have to know that I have waited so long to see you again," Aisling confessed.

"I know it's been hard. For me too, that's why we have to wait until the time is right. Then one day we could be together," Miles told her.

"You better go before someone sees you. Remember, I'm still a part of the clergy. I can't have the townspeople know about you, about us, and not about Sloane," Miles warned, as Aisling slipped out the side door of the Chapel and walked the few blocks home in the cold midnight air.

SLOANE

"Maybe one day, I will learn more about my father. My mother said so little about him that she often made up stories about him growing up," she told her new friend Abigail.

"I think he must live in a far, far away," Sloane told her.

"What makes you say that?"

"Whenever I bring him up, my mother makes some vague answer about him. I never get a straight answer," Sloane explained.
Deep down inside, she didn't know if any of her stories were true, but she also knew that someday she would meet him. When that someday might be was somewhere in the back of her mind. She couldn't think about that right now, but she often wondered why Miles was so close to her mother. In the months that they lived in Abington Square, Aisling had visited Miles almost every day. Sloane wondered how they could become so close so quickly. Her mother never became close to humans, as she remembered her mother say, *"Grandmother Sara would always say to trust a human would be a sin."* She couldn't put two and two together.

"What would make a man of the clergy want to spend time with a nurse, no less one who was with magical powers?" Sloan asked herself. She didn't understand it all, or even less, why the people in Abington Square were so against her and her mother. It wasn't like they were out to hurt anyone.

Sloane and Aisling settled into the small quaint town for one reason, to find refuge from judgment and a place to renew their faith, at least this is what her mother told her. If only she had known that she and Aisling were seen as the work of evil, they would have looked elsewhere. Sloane knew that she and her family didn't stand out among the townspeople. No one ever questioned them. They dressed the same as other townspeople did. They ate in the same restaurants and shopped in the same stores, but why now were they being questioned for being just like them. It was the reason why Aisling and Sloane were being called witches.

Chapter Six

ABIGAIL

Paige Chapel had all the beauty and luster of an Old English church. Its living quarters were decorated with the finest of silk linens. The nuns liked it that way, as they took to using blue, scarlet, and purple thread in their curtains, something is written in the Old Testament of the Bible. The eloquently styled gold fabric hung gently against the early 1900s style gothic windows. It's what Abigail loved most about living there.

Every night Abigail had chores to complete for the nuns. Her favorite being cooking most of their meals. Tonight she would make a bisque soup and fresh lobster dripping in butter sauce. Abigail prided herself in cooking for the nuns. She often thought that her calling would be in opening her restaurant someday, unlike Sloane, who wished to follow in the steps of her mother, Aisling. Being a nurse suited her; she didn't get sick at the sight of blood. She had a calmness about her that Abigail always admired about her.

At 5 pm, Abigail began the preparations for her bisque soup, heavy cream, and refined spices that she bought early in the morning. *"The nuns will love this recipe,"* she thought to herself as she put the finishing touches on dinner. Setting the long wooden table with soup bowls and dishes decorated with tiny lavender and yellow flowers, she took the pot of soup and began serving the nuns who began to enter the dining area.

"What is the special occasion," asked Sister Mary Thomas, taking a sip of her soup.

"No special occasion. Just a new recipe," answered Abigail, as she poured the remaining in Sister Mary Margaret's bowl.

Abigail watched with great satisfaction as the nuns ate with content. Ripping the pieces of Cape Cod bread and dipping it into their plates, she had such great satisfaction in her work, as time seemed to pass quickly before the nuns finished their meal and retreated out of the dining area to their rooms for prayer,

"I feel a terrible pain!" Sister Mary Margaret screamed as she held her stomach before striking her insides.

"What should we do?" asked Abigail.

"I don't know. Call Father Miles," answered Sister Mary Thomas, as Abigail ran to the phone.

"Hello," answered Miles.

"Father, please come quick! Sister Mary Margaret is ill!"

"I'm on my way," he responded nervously, as he rushed to get to the convent. Miles could hear the yells from Sister Mary Margaret's bedroom.

Laying lifeless on her floor, Sister Mary Margaret couldn't move, she felt helpless. Abigail hoped that it wasn't the soup or her delicately cooked lobster that she had spent hours preparing and making. No, it was more serious than that, as Sister Mary Margaret's body began to burn up with a fever.

"Put cold compresses on her," Miles directed, as Abigail took a soft white terrycloth towel and began soaking it in ice-cold water. Within less than seventy-two hours, but nothing seemed to help.

"She still has a high fever, Father," Abigail informed. "What do we do now?"

"I have someone who can help," he said, as he picked up the phone. "Hello, Aisling? We need you here at Paige Chapel. Sister Mary Margaret is sick, and we don't know what else to do."

"I'll be right there," she said with urgency in her voice.

Taking the short walk into town, Aisling and Sloane arrived at Paige Chapel. They entered the darkroom that contained nothing more than a bed and a small bouquet. On the nightstand was a Bible and a rosary made up of dried red rosebuds. Miles watched as Aisling mixed oils. "You must leave us alone," she told him. Closing the door behind him, Aisling put her hands on Sister Mary Margaret's body to ease the pain and fever that had consumed her body.

Down the hall, the nuns and Abigail waited impatiently for answers, as Kimberly combined a handful of Jasmine, honey, water, and various flower petals in a clay bowl before dumping it over her body with a dry cloth. The smell of the mixture filled the room, as they visualized health and light for Sister Mary Margaret. They visualized the healing of the fragile nun, as they touched her body with their hands since this seemed to short-circuit the effects of the fever and pain. Slowly, Aisling and Sloane watched as Sister Mary Margaret opened her eyes and sat up in bed. She hadn't been able to move for the last three days. Looking around the room, she had felt a sense of renewal before hurrying to get out of bed. She opened the door to her bedroom, where she found Miles, Abigail, and Sister Mary Thomas sitting in the quiet of the hallway between their rooms. They were astonished, even questioned, as if she had never been sick.

AISLING

Leaving the living quarters of Paige Chapel, Sloane and her mother walked back the short distance home. Aisling felt a sense of relief to be able to heal Sister Mary Margaret. Without saying much the walk home, they entered their cottage home was decorated with herbs and flowers. She hoped that the work that they were doing in Abington Square would distract the townspeople from their judgment. Although they moved to town so that Sloane could be closer to her father, Aisling didn't realize how harsh the people could be of newcomers. She was often asked questions as to her lifestyle. They often wondered what allowed her to heal people better than any physician in the area. Something wasn't quite right of her and her daughter, as rumors began to flare after hearing of Sister Mary Margaret's healing. It just served further suspicion of Aisling and Sloane.

MILES

"Why was it so important to close the door?" Miles thought to himself. He thought about their actions all day and night since Aisling and Sloane came to Paige Chapel. He had no answers, but he continued to hear the rumors of suspicion of their healing practices.

Miles wouldn't judge them. That wasn't what he was about as a man of the clergy. He decided that he wouldn't think about it any further. It was nonsense to believe that Aisling was a true witch. That was her grandmother Sara, but not her. They were completely different people. Entering the living quarters of the Chapel, Sister Mary Thomas welcomed him with cheer.

"So glad to see you, Father," she told him, opening the door.

"Good morning, sister. How is Sister Mary Margaret?"

"Wonderful, Father. Thank you for asking. She is already in the garden watering her plants."

Miles knew that she was back to her old self again. Sister Mary Margaret loved nothing more than to work in the Chapel's garden. Her

Hydrangeas were the most sought-after in all of Abington Square. Tourists came from all over to see these beautiful flowers.

"Father, I must ask. How does Nurse Aisling do it? How is she able to heal everyone?" Sister Mary Thomas asked with curiosity.

"I don't know. I don't know," he answered.
Closing the door behind him, they walked the rest of the way to the back garden, he thought about what Sister Mary Thomas had asked him. Aisling was the first person that he had ever trusted. There was no way that she would deceive him. She knew that he was a religious man.

Aisling wouldn't ever cross that line with him. From now on, his focus would be on Sloane and his work in the church. He wouldn't let a rumor get in the way of his feelings for them, and besides, if Aisling were a witch, wouldn't he had known it by now?
He needed to clear his head. Saying his goodbyes to Sister Mary Thomas and Sister Mary Margaret, he walked into the center of town to Fairchild's for a bite to eat. It was the last place that he wanted to visit. Most of the gossip was heard there, but it had the best food in town. Taking a seat at the counter, he turned over his cup to signal to the waitress for coffee.

"She's a witch I said," Miles overheard two older women in their 70s speak.

"I tell you there has to be something wrong with her. How can she heal someone so fast?" the first older woman questioned.

"I heard she instantly healed Sister Mary Margaret," answered the second older woman.

"No-she had been sick for days," she responded.

"She's a witch I tell you." Miles overheard the conversation of the two women, as he got up from his seat and paid for his coffee.

There was no way he could sit there listening to the lies that are told of Aisling. Maybe it wasn't the best idea for her and Sloane to live in Abington Square. People were too judgmental, too strict. He decided there was no other safe place to go but to return home.

Chapter Seven

ABIGAIL

Abigail was grateful to have a friend in Sloane. She didn't understand how Sloane and Aisling were able to heal everyone; she didn't worry about that; she didn't worry about the suspicious talk of the people in town. Walking into Fairchild's, Abigail overheard Dr. Matthew talking to the waitress.

"It's a miracle really," Dr. Matthew told her. "Like something out of a magic book of sorts."

"No one can understand how two women could heal Sister Mary Margaret so quickly," the waitress commented.

"It is amazing," said Dr. Matthews.

"I think it's more than that, people are coming in here saying they're witches, something evil," the waitress explained.

"Witches?" questioned Dr. Matthew.

"Yeah, a witch. There's something about them that doesn't seem right about them. I can't put my finger on it," the waitress replied, before walking away.

"People think they are witches?" Abigail thought to herself before leaving Fairchild's. She walked across Main Street and back to Paige Chapel.

"Abington Square was funny that way. Even anyone seemed just a little bit different from the rest; automatically, there had to be something evil about them," Abigail told her.

She wouldn't let them get to her. She was just happy to see Sister Mary Margaret back to herself again. Opening the recipe book, she quickly went through the pages in her book. She had settled on beef barley stew. She had made many times for the nuns, so she knew that no one would get sick on it. Taking out the pans and pots, Abigail began to make their meal. She imagined herself working in a high-end restaurant and cooking extravagant orders. A beep on her phone signaled that Sloane was texting her.

"Did you hear the rumors?" she asked.

"No, what?" Abigail answered.

"People in town think that mom and I are witches? Witches?!" The thought had crossed her mind but didn't believe it.

"Why would anyone think that about you?" she texted. A second later, Sloane responded, "Sister Mary Margaret. We may have to leave."

Abigail's heart began to sink at the thought of her best friend moving. She was the only friend she had in Abington Square. So what if people thought that they were witches. They wouldn't hurt a soul. Why do the people have to punish Sloane and Aisling? Why do they have to punish her? Abigail felt the heat of anger overpower her, as she tried to focus on dinner. It was ridiculous. Not even the nuns had expressed their fear that they were witches. They would have been the first to say so. At half-past six, Sister Mary Thomas and Sister Mary Margaret had sat down to eat dinner. Beef barley stew with buttered rolls. Abigail gleamed a smile at how much the nuns had liked her food.

"One day, you will be a chef. A wonderful chef in Abington Square," Sister Mary Thomas told her.

It was Abigail's dream to one day become a chef, but now wasn't the time for career thinking. She had more important things to think about. She couldn't help but wonder if the nuns believed that Sloane and Aisling were witches. Were they the ones who started the rumor? Immediately, she dismissed the thought. Besides, they were nuns; it wouldn't be in their character.

SLOANE

Sloane wondered how much longer she and Aisling would able to stay in Abington Square. She had finally made her first best friend in Abigail. It would be difficult to find someone like her in life again. She watched as her mother cooked together with a mixture of fruit flowers and honey. The aroma was good enough to eat. Carefully, she watched as Aisling stirred the mixture over and over for the right consistency. With a tablespoon of honey another pair of fruit flowers, Sloane worked with her mother to learn all that there was to heal people.

It seemed that every day another and another person was getting sick. Fevers with high temperatures went rampant across the town. Dr. Matthew Carney was the town's physician. An older man in his early sixties, he had lived his whole life in Abington Square. He lived in the same eighteenth-century home that his parents purchased when he was ten years old. He never left the old home, not even to go to college. He loved this home, the richly decorated antique tables, and lamps, the Persian sofas that added class and flare to it. He would never leave this house, not for anything or anyone. When he began practicing as a physician, his parents had already passed away. They never had the chance to see him graduate. That alone forced him to find a way to stay in Abington Square.

Shortly after graduating, he rented a small office over Fairchild's and opened his first practice. The office didn't look like much, just a waiting room filled with chairs, magazines, and books. Dr. Matthew didn't care. He didn't become a physician to impress anyone. Renting an office on the north side of Abington Square allowed him to be in the center of town. He would often see a handful of people in a week, but now his office was packed with patients. They all complained of the same symptoms, a fever of 103 and pain throughout their bodies. At first, Dr. Matthew, as the people called him, thought it was the flu, but soon came to realize that none of the antibiotics given were working. He feared that something greater was happening. Maybe a disease without a cure. For those that Dr. Matthew couldn't help, he referred them to Aisling hoping that patients would get better. A little of this and a little of that, the aroma of honey filled the homes of Abington Square.

Using the last of the ingredients in the cabinet, Aisling and Sloane walked the two blocks into town to purchase more honey. Next door to Fairchild's was Abington Square Convenience Store. Their shelves stocked to the brim with fine ingredients, gourmet spreads, and chess. Aisling and her daughter entered the store to

"You are a witch." Aisling overheard someone saying.

"A witch, is that what people believe that I am?" She continued to walk up and down the aisles of the store.

Swiftly, more and more townspeople began to move out of aisles or out of the store completely. Fear was rapidly filling the town. Walking up to the checkout counter, Aisling paid for her groceries. She and Sloane carried the bags out of the store and turned left past Fairchild's *"there they are,"* Aisling overheard a young man tell a group of friends standing outside. *"She's a witch!"*

Walking fast through the center of town, Aisling walked the two blocks back home. She couldn't help but feel that she was a target of something bigger.

"A witch, that's what they keep calling us. I am not a witch!" she told herself, as she walked with great vigor back into the house.

Chapter Eight

ABINGTON SQUARE

Every first Monday of the month, people within the town of Abington Square came together to discuss issues. Taxes, town improvements, and anything related to the upkeep of the homes. Tonight it would be different. Tonight, what was on the minds of the people was to protect their small community. They wouldn't let anyone ruin it. Miles entered the town hall in the back of the room, a few seats away from Sister Mary Thomas and Sister Mary Margaret. Abigail was also with them. She didn't go to many meetings, but she thought that it might be important to listen to what happened at these meetings. One month it got so bad that Dr. Matthew almost stepped down. Some people I guess get too emotional and don't know how to control their tempers. Tonight, people were loudly chattering until the meeting had come to order.

"Order ... order!" Still, the noise was loud.

"Order...order!" he yelled again and again until everyone turned their attention to him.

Dr. Matthew was the town's keeper. He didn't want the job, since it was political. But he felt strongly for Abington Square and its people to leave it to someone else. The first order of business was the tourist committee. Sister Mary Margaret was thrilled to hear the news of a place where she could be her talents to work in town.

"Forget the tourists!" yelled a member of the community. Dr. Matthew, at first, couldn't hear the noise.

"What was that?" Silence filled the room. Not a sound. It was so quiet that it was deafening. "Forget the gardening!" the voice said again.

"What would you like to discuss? It is important to preserving Abington Square," the voice said again. Dr. Matthew explained.

"We want to talk about the witch!" yelled another voice. Miles looked up toward the voice that was speaking.

"We have a witch in Abington Square!" yelled another voice.

Abigail looked around the room, "they can't be talking about Sloane and her mom," she thought to herself.

"That witch in town healed my wife," said another.

"Mine too. That woman and her daughter, honey and potions, all kinds of wicked stuff," yelled yet another.

Dr. Matthew had no idea how to handle this kind of talk. A witch in Abington Square, say it isn't so. Abigail's eyes moved across the room. She hoped that Sister May Thomas and Sister Mary Margaret wouldn't say a word. It would be out of character for them to talk so harshly about another person.

"It is evil in town!" yelled another person, before everyone in the room began to get out of control. There was no way for Dr. Matthew to calm such noise.

"Order! Order!" he tried with all his might. "Can we please have order!" he yelled.

Dr. Matthew knew that they were talking about Aisling and Sloane. He could see the dark expression that overshadowed Miles's face, as the meeting ended. There was no sense in holding a meeting when people were this emotional.

MILES

After the evening's town meeting, Miles thought hard about Aisling and Sloane. *"I have to protect them,"* he thought, as he walked and walked down the Victorian lite streets, the sunlight catching a glimmer of the fall foliage from the trees. He took Seymour to Munster and down Orchard and found himself at the front steps of Aisling's home. He walked up to the steps and rang the doorbell. No one answered. He rang the doorbell again, but when no one answered, he tried to unlock the door.

"Hello!" he yelled up.

"Upstairs," yelled Aisling's voice, as she came down the second-floor steps. She was surprised to see him, "What are you doing here so late?" she asked.

"It's only 8:30," he answered.

"On a school night?" she joked, as she took a seat on a solid oak rocking chair.

"You have to leave," he told her. In shock, at first, she wasn't sure what to say.

"Leave, why? Why would I need to leave?" Miles couldn't believe that she didn't know why this had to be some joke.

"Don't you see how many people in town want to hurt you? They are calling you a witch. A true-life witch!" Aisling hung on to every word that he was saying.

"I'm not a witch, Miles. You know that I'm not. I shouldn't have to leave because of other people's fears. I'm flesh and blood just like you," she reminded him. Taking a seat on the sofa next to her. His eyes looked up at the second-floor stairs. Instantly, she could read his mind.

"She's not home," Aisling assured him.

"I'm worried. You and Sloane came here to be closer to me. Now everyone in town is questioning your motives. They are questioning your healing ability. I'm freaking out here," he got up from his seat.

"I'm not leaving, Miles. I haven't done anything wrong. The town bully won't challenge me," she told him as she got up from her seat and opened the front door.

"Go home and rest, Miles. Tomorrow is a new day. You will see things clearer."

Walking down the front steps of Aisling's home, he took a walk back to Paige Chapel. Opening the heavy Mahogany doors, he took a seat in a pew and began to pray:

"Lord, I'm weary. My energy is sagging, and my motivation is lagging. And I am so in need of you. I need your strength and your fresh touch to get back on track again. Your Word says the joy of the Lord is my strength," Miles took a pause.

"If that's true, then I need your joy to replace all the bone-tired parts of my mind, body, and soul. I'm tired of feeble efforts. Lord, I want to mount up with wings like an eagle and not just fly. I want to soar." Miles thought hard about Aisling and Sloane, more than he ever had in all his years.

Miles sat in the darkness of the small chapel, He hoped to gain the strength and the answers to help Aisling and Sloane. He wouldn't stand for hurt feelings. They wouldn't accuse them of doing evil. Maybe Aisling was right. Tomorrow is a new day. He could hear her words so confident in his head. Getting up, he returned to his study to think.

Chapter Nine

ABIGAIL

Abigail watched Sloane as she sat quietly at the kitchen table of the living quarters. The bubbliest person in Abington Square was at a loss for words. Abigail couldn't explain it. She wanted to bring up the town hall meeting but knew it would only make her quieter. Maybe she already knew about their talk of witches. Their secret potions and sweet smells of honey filled the rooms of patients. After hearing the crowds of comments made tonight, she started to question her support for Sloane. If she was a witch, there was no way that she could stay friends with her. How could she, Sister Mary Thomas and Sister Mary Margaret, be the closest thing that she had to the family? She had no one else, but she couldn't just sit there and not say a word.

"Something wrong?" Sloane didn't say a word. Her eyes glazed in thought, Abigail prepared for her best friend to at least say something. "People can be mean," Sloane told her.

"People stink, Sloane." She watched as Sloane's blue eyes became fierce with anger.

"They think my mom and I are witches. Do you think that I'm a witch?!"

Abigail was now the one to sit quietly. She didn't want to tell the truth, but all the mixtures of oils and their ability to heal anyone started to make her think twice. She started to believe what everyone did about their magical powers.

"You're not answering, Abigail. Now I believe you think that my mom and I are witches. You of all people! The one person that I thought I could trust. You're a fake just like the rest of them. You're no true friend, you're a hypocrite!" she yelled before storming off.

"Sloane- wait. That's not true. I never said that I believed them. Come back!" she yelled, but it was too late.

Sloane had made it out of the living quarters and around the corner to her home. The loud yelling startled Sister Mary Thomas out of the living room and into the kitchen. She could tell how upset Abigail was feeling.

"Everything okay?" Abigail looked at her with tears in her eyes. No, no, everything isn't okay. I've had a terrible fight with Sloane.

Going up to her bedroom, she picked up her cell phone to text her, but what could she say? *"I still believe you, but I'm afraid that your hocus pocus magic will punish me."* She didn't know how to reverse the damage, because even she started to question Sloane and Aisling, and so she wrote: *"can we talk?"* Silence. There was no answer. Abigail waited and waited, but still, there was no answer.

AISLING

Storming through the front door, Aisling was sitting on the living room couch. She wondered what was making her daughter so mad. "Sloane- what happened?" Going towards the second-floor steps, she turned to her mother. Tears were streaming down her eyes.

"We're witches!" Confused, Aisling had no idea had to answer.

"Who's a witch?" She waited for her daughter to answer, a beep from her cell phone signaled that she had gotten a message.
It was the fifth message that Abigail had sent her, but she didn't want to talk to her anymore. She had nothing left to say.
"Everyone thinks that we are witches. The townspeople, Abigail, the nuns, no one believes that we are innocent."

Sloane ran up the rest of the stairs toward her bedroom, took her cell phone, and dunked it into a glass of water that was sitting next to her bed. That would teach her. Now she could never contact her.
Aisling could hear the slam of Sloane's door. She took a seat back down on the couch. Not sure who she could trust she thought to call Miles. He would know what to do.

Chapter Ten

MILES

A long night was ahead of him, as he thought about Aisling and Sloane. Maybe it wasn't safe for them to stay in Abington Square. He thought about leaving and taking them with him, but how would he explain, leaving Paige Chapel, and it would only fuel the rumors that they were witches. It was a tough decision, and he wouldn't have the answers in one night, not even two or three. No, it would take time to figure out the best plan of action for everyone to be happy.

Opening his Bible, he heard a knock on the door. He walked towards the front door and called out, "Who is it ... Aisling?" a muffled voice answered back.

"I'm sorry to bother you, Father Miles." It was Dr. Matthew at his door.

"We need to talk?" he asked Miles.

"Something wrong?" Dr. Matthew didn't know how to explain what he was feeling.

"I'm not sure. After the town hall meeting, a bunch of townspeople got together with a plan to go over Aisling and Sloane. They fear that they are witches. They fear that their evil will destroy Abington Square." Miles listened intently to Dr. Matthew, and he knew that he had to protect them from the people.

"Do you believe that they are witches?" Miles bluntly asked him. After a long silence, Dr. Matthew thought about his question.

"I think that we are playing with fire, Father Miles. If we let it go, something terrible may happen." Miles didn't believe that Aisling and Sloane were anything more than just talented nurses. Dismissing the thought that anything was wrong, Dr. Matthew left with a warning, do something to prove that they weren't evil or they will have no choice but to face the consequences.

Returning to his Bible, he knelt on his knees to pray from Psalm 59:

"Save me from my enemies, my God; protect me from those who attack me! Save me from those evil people; rescue me from those murderers! Look! They are waiting to kill me; cruel people are gathering against me. It is not because of any sin or wrong I have done, nor because of any fault of mine, O Lord, that they hurry to their places.
Rise, Lord God Almighty, and come to my aid; see for yourself, God of Israel!" Miles closed his Bible and began to think about Aisling and Sloane.

"I can't lose them again. I will do everything I can to protect them. A promise is a promise, and I promised Aisling that I would protect them," Miles told himself.

He felt like his heart was being ripped apart into pieces. Miles put his face into his hands and began to tear up. His eyes began to fill up like buckets of water. He cried so loud that the neighbors could feel his pain. Miles had never cried so hard.

ABIGAIL

She waited all night to hear from Sloane. She had sent five text messages, which was more than what she wanted to send. Still, she heard nothing.

Abigail feared the worse. She feared that Sloane would get so mad at her that she would cast a spell against her. Worse, she feared she lost her best friend. Abigail wondered if there was some potion that could be mixed to bring Sloane back. She thought about the fact that they were best friends since Kindergarten. *"Remember, you swore not to tell a soul. We are soul sisters."* Sloane's words stung her. She always remembered the promise, but she never thought about keeping secrets about witches and potions. Abigail wished Sloane would answer her. She wished that she would answer all the questions that Abigail had for her. If only she could prove that there was a good explanation for everything that she had heard and seen. The healing of Sister Mary Margaret, the smell of honey, and the hidden mixtures that she carried in her bag. Abigail wanted to believe her, but right now, she just couldn't, as her tears turned from sorrow to anger. She knew that she shouldn't be angry with Sloane, but she wasn't giving any other reason to feel at the moment.

SLOANE

Sloane couldn't remember the last time that she was this angry. Opening the tall, tiny closet in her bedroom, she reached for an old tattered book that sat at the top of her shelf. Taking the book, she blew the pile of dust that sat on top of it. She remembered the day that her grandmother Sara gave it to her. *Take good care of it. Don't let anyone else near it. It has the magic you need to survive in this world.* Sloane will never forget those words. Opening up the pages, she found a bookmark left by her grandmother. The page had a marker with a heading that said *Potions*. She softly touched the pages so as not to rip them. There was one that used toads and rabbits. She could never use one with animals. A few pages more, she found what she was looking for, a potion to change a person's heart. Maybe this is what was needed to change the hearts and thoughts of

Abigail and the townspeople. Maybe then they would accept her and her mother as being human beings.

Running down the flight of steps to the kitchen, she took out the heavy black pot that she used for large batches of mixtures. Aisling could hear her opening cabinets and taking ingredients out and putting them into the big black pot. Getting up from her chair, she walked into the kitchen and saw her mother's potion box. "Sloane, please, don't do anything that you will regret." She didn't listen. Opening the back door, she walked down the three steps and into the grass where she found rocks and sticks to bum a fire. Lifting the heavy pot, she placed it in the middle of the stones. She began to pour cloves, honey, and other oils and herbs. A strong aroma began to fill the air. Aisling soon followed her into the yard.

"Are you sure about this?" she said with skepticism. A nod from Sloane assured her that this had to use the spell.

"Tousles, stoles, and drops, we must begin to change their hearts." Together they said these words over and over until the sunny blue skies began to tum a dark blackish gray.

The sound of their voices began to raise, as their next-door neighbor, an elderly couple in their eighties peered through their window. Their eyes are growing wide; they quickly shuttered their blinds and curtains. Stirring the pot in a clockwise direction, so to not reverse their spell, *"Tousles, stoles, and drops, we must begin to change their hearts."* It was then that their energies were released. They repeated until the roar of thunder began, the heavy winds and rain came storming down on them. Abington Square would never be the same. The aroma of the pot filled the air, as Aisling and Sloane watched their potion glisten in the damp midnight air.

ABINGTON SQUARE

The rains began to hit the town harder and harder. Dr. Matthew retreated to his office, a small crack of his window opened, an unknown smell seeped into his window. He couldn't decipher what it was, but he was more worried about the torrential rain that was coming down. There weren't any weather reports of a flood, not even a storm. Just a minute ago, the crisp fall air and bright sunny skies had felt good coming into his window, but he was now beginning to worry. The rain wasn't letting up, as he closed his window and watched from his second-floor office.

Instead, it was getting more dangerous. At the comer, two well-dressed businessmen stood under the awning at Fairchild's. They had just finished having a business lunch when the wind gained speed. The water from the rain reached as high as the awning and swept the two men up. Dr. Matthew watched as their bodies were swept away down the flooded main street. His body was going numb, and he couldn't move. Thick smoke began to cover Abington Square. He could no longer see out his window. It was something that he had never experienced.

Across town, Sister Mary Thomas and Sister Mary Margaret felt the rumble of thunder settle over the living quarters of Paige Chapel. The loud noise startled them, as the lights began to flicker on and off. Abigail, who sat next to her bedroom window, watched the rain fall heavily onto the ground.

Miles closed the pages of his Bible; he looked out his study window. He watched as the rain was pouring down. A streak of light ran across the sky, and the clouds opened up to give way to buckets of water. It wasn't just any ole' rainstorm. It was a curse. He walked away from the window and opened his Bible and began to read Psalm 13,

"Consider and answer me, O Lord my God. Give light (life) to my eyes, or I will sleep the sleep of death, and my enemy will say, I have overcome him, And my adversaries will rejoice when I am shaken. But I have trusted and relied on and been confident in Your lovingkindness and faithfulness. My heart shall rejoice and delight in your salvation," Miles could feel his heart again grow heavy.

Miles knew that the town was plagued. At that moment, he knew that trouble was ahead. Picking up his phone, he called Aisling. The phone rang and rang, but no one answered. He began to worry that something might have happened. His greatest fear was that they disappeared, then he would never see them again. The townspeople were wicked that way. They had fearful hearts and found it difficult to forgive. Putting on his raincoat, he knew the best thing to do was to go to Aisling's house. He didn't bother bringing a raincoat, it was too heavy of rain for that, as he opened the door. A strong smell reached the inside of his nose. The smell was so powerful that he quickly closed the door and stayed in his study. He would wait until the rain stopped, but if he did, it might be too late. He walked back to the front door, held his breath, and ran the whole way to Aisling's home.

Chapter Eleven

AISLING

Running around the large puddles of rain that filled the town's streets, Miles went up to the front steps and rang the doorbell. Silence, there was no answer. Hitting the doorbell over again, silence, there was no answer. He looked through the dark windows that showed no sign that anyone was home. He watched as the second streak of lightning lit the sky. Smoke filled the back of the house. A fire, was that why Aisling didn't answer the phone? Miles ran to the back of the house. He was shocked by what he was seeing. Dressed in a black shawl that covered her body. Her long flowing red hair tied in a bun, Aisling stood next to her daughter. *Tousles, stoles, and drops, we must begin to change their hearts.* He listened to them chant this over and over again. Miles didn't know what to say. He didn't know if he should go or begin to pray. He knew that without the full armor of God on him, he would wait to say anything. Remembering Psalm 143, he whispered,

"Hear my prayer, O Lord, Listen to my supplications! My heart grows numb within me. I remember the days of old; I meditate on all that you have done; I ponder the work of your hands. I reach out my hands to you; my throat thirsts for you, as a parched land [thirsts for water]. Selah," Miles turned to put on his coat and walked out of Paige Chapel.

A third and fourth streak of lightning flashed across the sky, before calm filled the sky. The rain ceased immediately and gave way to the bright sunny skies that Abington Square had before the storm. Aisling turned her head to find Miles standing there. She had no words left to say. She and her daughter were witches, and now there was no denying her secret.

Miles said nothing to Aisling and Sloane. He walked out of the backyard and into the center of town. Aisling's eyes followed him. Aisling knew that Miles knowing her secret, meant it was all over for them. Sloane would never know her father, and she would never forgive her mother for following her grandmother's path to witchcraft.

MILES

Miles walked down through the center of town. The eighteenth-century restaurants and boutiques that fashioned Abington Square looked different to him now. He had a big decision to make; he had to decide to turn over Aisling and Sloane to the townspeople. It was wrong, and a priest, he had no place defending evil.

"Father Miles!" His name disturbed his thinking; it was Dr. Matthew leaving his office.

"I thought for sure I would be stuck here all night. That was some rain, thunder, and lightning. That smell? Did you get a whiff of it?"

Miles didn't know what to say. He knew that the truth would have to come out. There was no way he could hold onto such a secret, but then again, it wasn't a secret anymore.

"Listen, Dr. Matthew; we need to talk, but not here, not now." Dr. Matthew could see the seriousness in Miles's face.

"Okay, sure. You name the time and place, and I'll be there." Miles's eyes told a thousand stories in them. Dr. Matthew watched his expression as he nodded and said, "Great! I will call you soon to set something up."

Miles continued to walk down the emptiness of the streets, as Dr. Matthew watched him. He knew that he was carrying a heavy burden, but Miles didn't know how to tell him. Taking a long way home, Miles entered the side door and into his study and sulked in an antique velvet chair.

Soaked from the rain, he couldn't take the image out of his head of Aisling and Sloane chanting over that large black pot. It was surreal to him. He thought for sure Aisling would have tried to call him, but she didn't. He had suspected something wasn't completely right with her. She always had a weird way about her, but he never imagined that she would be a witch, or if anything, that she was a practicing one. For years, he knew that Aisling's mother Sara was just evil. She would walk through the house, saying phrases, and would run from the sight of garlic. Miles thought that maybe she was just too wired, but he didn't think that she was into witchcraft. If he knew it, he would have prayed with her.

ABIGAIL

Abigail opened up the window of her bedroom and listened to the chirping of the birds in the trees. If it weren't for the wet sidewalks and streets, no one would have ever thought that torrential rain had hit Abington Square. Five days had passed, and Sloane still didn't return her text. She couldn't remember when they had ever gone that long without talking. It was over, she thought to herself. All of the years that they had spent together since kindergarten proved to be nothing. *Remember, you swore not to tell a soul. We are soul sisters.* Were they? Were they ever really soul sisters? Abigail didn't think so. It was all just a lie. She could never trust her again, and she wouldn't. "Abigail-is everything okay?" It was Sister Mary Thomas checking in on her. It was three o'clock in the afternoon; there was no time to give Sloane a second thought. It was time to make dinner.

She opened the door to her bedroom and down the steps into the kitchen. It was time for new beginnings for her; there was no more sorrow or pain. She wouldn't think about Sloane, her mother, or the fact that probably worshipped the Devil. That wasn't her scene. She was a devout Christian, and she was proud of it. Every Sunday she went to church with Sister Mary Thomas and Sister Mary Margaret. Soon she would start college, culinary school to be exact. Maybe instead of opening a fancy restaurant, she would open a soup kitchen.

Taking out the salmon from the refrigerator that she had defrosted overnight, she began to whip the finest of mashed potatoes. Creamy, they melted in the sisters' mouths. Abigail would change her focus from now on. Now the focus would be on her and serving others.

AISLING

Aisling and Sloane carried the large black pot that they used to cook the potion back into the house. There was no reason to hide their witchcraft since Miles had seen them. It would be just a matter of time before the Town Keeper, Dr. Matthew would show up at their front door accusing them of evil. Miles was a good man, a good and faithful servant. That was why she was so surprised that he would have any interest in her. As soon as Miles met Aisling's mother Sara, she thought for sure it would be over, but it wasn't at all. It took Miles to get through seminary to decide that the relationship wasn't right for him. He couldn't serve two people, both her and God. He had to make a choice, even though Sloane was just a newborn. He chose God,

Aisling knew that then and she knew that now. She would never dream of telling him what to do, but he also didn't ever witness to her. Perhaps he didn't know what to say once he met her mother. She was a pure witch, unlike Aisling, who only did it to please her. So instead,

Aisling and Miles went their separate ways. They were different people who wanted different things in life. That was the thinking that got her through each day that he was gone. Aisling turned to her mother Sara for support, who assured her that witches had no business being with humans, and she was right.

SLOANE

For the first time in years, Sloane felt invigorated. She felt free to have control over people, this is what she thought of life, and she didn't care who knew it. Going back upstairs to her room, she held her grandmother's potion book close to her. She opened the tattered pages and flipped through them. She spent hours closing herself away from the world to read every page thoroughly. Sloane didn't want to miss a word. Not one potion or mixture that could give her the power to take over Abington Square. That was her goal. The fight with Abigail was a rude awakening for her. She should have never trusted a mortal human to keep secrets, let alone to give her trust. Humans were just that, untrustworthy, just like grandma Sara had told her, *"to trust a human would be a sin. To trust in human power would be an even bigger sin. You have the power to overtake everyone. Use my book, and you will have anything that you want from this world."*

Thinking about these words gave her great distress. Aisling missed her grandmother and her wise words so much. She may have seemed strange to some, but to Aisling, she was her everything. She would follow in her footsteps and become just like her. Aisling would no longer act like humans. Instead, she would devout herself to the power that she gave to her patients.

Chapter Twelve

ABINGTON SQUARE

As the rains had subsided and the wet sidewalks and streets dried up, the town of Abington Square began to fill up with people. Fairchild's had seen a crowd of people that they hadn't seen in years, but it wasn't for the hot coffee and brown sugar pancakes. Instead, it was to talk about the storm and their fear of evil entering their town.

"Never saw so much rain," said a middle-aged woman in her fifties.

"No one has. Took two businesspeople away, right in front of Fairchild's and down to no man's land," said another.

"Where did you hear that story?" asked the middle-aged woman. "It's not a story. It's the truth. Dr. Matthew saw it with his very eyes," as the townspeople began to speak fanatically.

"It's those witches I tell you. Those women on Orchard. They are punishing us," they all agreed.

"If we don't get them out of here soon, we're all going to become like those two businessmen or worse; we'll be dead. Taken away from the Devil himself."

Taking to the brown sugar pancakes, it seemed like the orders wouldn't let up. Maybe it was their nerves getting the best of them, but their appetites grew bigger. Stacks and stacks of pancakes and large cups of coffee were being ordered all out of fear. Hearing the jingle of the store bell, Dr. Matthew took a seat in the crowded restaurant and read the menu. He didn't need to, he had eaten there so many times, but today he would pretend not to know a thing. He wasn't sure how to handle what had happened yesterday.

As the Town Keeper, he was responsible for the people. A beep on his phone signaled he had a new message. It was Miles, the message read, *"Can we meet in your office this afternoon?* Dr. Matthew wrote back, *the sooner you get here, the better."* He sensed that trouble would be ahead after hearing the conversations of the townspeople inside Fairchild's. If he didn't make a decision soon, someone else would. Leaving his appetite for a later time, he walked back out of the crowded restaurant and walked the few steps back to his office, and besides, he would rather order out.

MILES

Dr. Matthew had just finished with his last patient for the morning. He took the magazines that were around the waiting area and put them into neat piles before Miles came in. He was a neat freak as some in town had called him. He liked to see things in order and became uneasy around confrontation. That's why it was so odd that he would have become the Town Keeper where there was always an argument or problem that would arise. The clock struck noon on the grandfather clock that sat in his office. Miles would be here soon.

Walking back and forth to finish some overdue paperwork, Dr. Matthew heard the creek of the patient waiting room door open up. It must be the Father. He was right on time. "Hello!" The voice didn't sound familiar.

"Dr. Matthew!" Walking out of his office to see who it was Abigail was standing before him.

"Hello, Abigail. I wasn't expecting you. Are you sick? Or did you have an appointment and I forget to put in my schedule?" he watched the door waiting any moment for Miles to walk in.

"No, no nothing like that but I do need to speak with you." The timing couldn't be more off.

"Well-normally I would, but it just so happens that I'm waiting for someone to come in. Could we make it for another time?" Her heart sank with disappointment, but she knew she should have called first.

"It's fine. I can come back later," she told him.

Opening the door to Dr. Matthew's office, Abigail had just missed Miles. Good thing too, the last thing that he wanted was for Abigail to see Miles coming in after hours. Then for sure rumors would be sparked around town. He had enough to deal with regarding the talk of goblins and potions. Dr. Matthew decided instead to wait for Miles out in the waiting area, just in case someone else tried to come in, as he could hear the creek of the waiting room door had opened, Miles started to walk in.

"I hope that I didn't keep you waiting. It was a mad scene outside. Townspeople are holding signs about evil," he explained.

"I was afraid that this would happen, but I knew that the people were too outspoken to wait for me to make any decisions," Dr. Matthew told him. The truth is, Miles was going to be the one to address the people, as he explained it all to him.

"Should we go in my office?" he offered Miles.

"It may be best. I have something— some serious things that I must tell with you." Worry filled Dr. Matthew's eyes as they walked into his office to sit down.

"I made my life mission always to be truthful. To uphold the Word and to be a servant to the people, but these past few weeks have tested my faith." Dr. Matthew listened with intent. He wasn't surprised that the town clergyman was having difficulty, but what he was surprised about was that he was telling him.

"I've known Aisling and Sloane for many years." Dr. Matthew became intrigued by this news. "But before I tell you anything, you must know that I had nothing to do with what happened yesterday. I wasn't involved in any of it, even though I witnessed it with my own eyes. I must tell you as the Town Keeper, the justice of the Abington Square, that I'm Sloane's father." Shock and surprise-filled his Dr. Matthew's face. Miles could see this as he tried not to react.

"How long have you known this?" He asked Miles.

"I don't mean to prey, and I'm not sure what has to lead you to confide in me, but I feel honored." Miles realized that this wasn't just any normal conversation.

"I had to get it off my chest. I've known you the longest. Remember, ten years ago that I told you that I had a child before entering the seminary?" Dr. Matthew nodded with a yes.
He remembered that conversation. He and Father Clancy had lunch together after service on a Sunday afternoon. It was the beginning of their friendship together, but why was he bringing it up now, especially with a witch hunt ahead.

"Aisling was my girlfriend at the time. She had Sloane just before I left for seminary. She knew that my heart was in the church, but her mother Sara did strange things."

"Strange things?" Dr. Matthew was intrigued.

"Yes, she would run from garlic. She kept oils and foods that she would mix and sprinkle all around the house. At that time in life, I didn't think too deeply about it. I figured she was just some woman who was losing her mind but after seeing Aisling and Sloane with that big black pot. I see things differently." Dr. Matthew couldn't believe that he had seen this and waited to tell someone.

"You saw it?" Miles dropped his head down toward the floor and then looked up. He swallowed hard. "I saw it with my own eyes. The black shawl, the smoke that came from the pot, but also the chanting that was being said. I had to wake up and realize that everything that the townspeople were saying was completely true. They are witches, people who follow evil. As the minister of Paige Chapel, I can't allow this to affect our community."

Dr. Matthew was impressed by Miles's strength. It took a lot for a man to turn away from flesh and blood.

"Are you willing to turn them in?" Clancy paused for a moment before saying, "Justice will happen for the people of Abington Square."

Opening the door to Dr. Matthew's waiting room, he stepped out into the crowded street. The people wanted justice too. Miles knew it, and so did Dr. Matthew. He watched Miles walk across the street until he couldn't see him any longer. He had a decision to be made, but not to prosecute. No that was the easy part, but rather how they would do it.

Abington Square had fewer rules than most of the surrounding areas. They could throw them away forever, or they could burn them at the stake. Time would only tell what will happen to Aisling and her daughter. He was glad that he didn't need to make that decision. He would leave it up to the church; yes, the church would bring justice after all.

ABIGAIL

Abigail walked the remaining blocks to the living quarters. She couldn't believe that she had the guts enough to walk into Dr. Matthew's office without an appointment, no less to tell him about Sloane and her mother. She didn't know how she would tell him that she suspected them of witchcraft since the night they healed Sister Mary Margaret, but she would. She would figure out the right time to turn them in. It was the only fair thing to do now that she and Sloane were no longer friends.

Remember, you swore not to tell a soul. We are soul sisters. That wasn't a friendship. Finally, after so many years, she would expose Sloane and her secret. Gone were the days of Kindergarten. Abigail wouldn't be afraid of her casting a spell on her. Let her work her magic. She would see that her powers were no good here in Abington Square and she would outcast like the rest of the people who tried to do her wrong.

Chapter Thirteen

AISLING

Aisling worried that what Miles had seen may have been too much for him. She never outright told him about her family. She knew that it would just chase him away. But her mother warned her to stop trusting humans. Didn't she realize that she was in a league of her own? Aisling knew why she trusted Miles so much. It was his faith that drew her to him, but the fact that he was Sloane's father. Aisling didn't want her holding hard feelings toward her for not being a traditional mother. Aisling missed her roots. Sara had taught at a young age about powerful magic. They held meetings with others who held the same power in a hidden church that was empty. They practiced magic for hours, dividing mixtures, and learning the chants of spells that defused heartache and pain.

They weren't bad witches. She was never taught to do wrong with her power. That's why it was so out of touch for Sloane to initiate her spell, but she didn't stop her either. Aisling knew she did it out of desperation. Should she call Miles and explain? No, it was too late for that. She saw his disappointment and shock in his expressions. She wouldn't bother him. She would wait to hear from him again. She thought of her mother's final words: *"to trust a human would be a sin. To not trust in human power would be an even bigger sin."*

MILES

Miles paced back and forth on the soft woven rug of his study. He couldn't contact Aisling or Sloane again, that was definitely for sure. Tomorrow would be the hardest day for him, but it would also start the dawning of a new day. It was difficult to get through the crowds of signs and townspeople yelling, *"Burn them at stake!"* The thought of it burned a hole in his stomach, but he knew that the townspeople wouldn't settle for just anything. They wanted justice and justice they would get. A knock on the door signaled that Dr. Matthew and the town watchmen were here to take Aisling and Sloane into custody. Miles wondered if they would resist or go peacefully. He believed that they would go in peace, in honor of Sara and what she taught them.

The cold rush of air blew through the linen curtains of Aisling's home. She closed her eyes and envisioned herself in chains. These humans would take her and Sloane away. They would punish them for being witches. All the good that they had done to heal the townspeople didn't help them. The people saw them as demonic, an evil presence in Abington Square.

A firm knock on the door caused Aisling to open her eyes. A second knock brought Sloane down from the second floor to the living room.

"Open up Aisling. I know you're in there," Miles warned them. Silence. The rush of weight sprung open the door, as the watchmen struggled to handcuff Aisling and Sloane.

"Don't fight." She warned her daughter. Go in peace. They have nothing on us but suspicion.

Taking Aisling and Sloane into the Abington Square Courthouse, the watchmen chained their arms and legs to the wall to keep their spirits from causing them to escape. Dr. Matthew walked around Abington Square posting signs of the trial for all the townspeople to attend. He had to since it was their right to be there. There was no use in having a trial if the people wouldn't be there.

ABIGAIL

Abigail had spent the whole day cooking and preparing Sister Mary Thomas and Sister Mary Margaret's meal. She was tired and weary from the four-course meal that she had prepared for Sister Mary Thomas's birthday. Stuffed mushrooms as an appetizer, a fresh chef's salad of kale and butternut squash, roasted lamb with mint jelly, and strawberry pie with vanilla ice cream. All of Sister Mary Thomas's favorites. After cleaning up the kitchen, she wanted nothing more than to take a walk through town. She had been in the kitchen for hours, and the break before dinner time would do her some good. She took her fall jacket and began to venture out toward Fairchild's. It seemed like a ghost town. Not at all filled with its usual sights of people talking and shopping for a Saturday afternoon. Instead, it felt cold and unwelcoming. There were signs posted everywhere. She wondered what was happening. Maybe a street fair, she always enjoyed them, as she walked inside the Abington Square market to purchase a gallon of milk for the homemade ice cream, she stopped to read a sign. *"Public Trial All to Attend!"* The public trial, she thought to herself. She continued to read further the names of those on the poster, *"Aisling and Sloane Turnberry."* Abigail took the poster off of the store window and brought it back to show Sister Mary Thomas and Sister Mary Margaret.

"Look ... Sisters! She showed the poster to them. "Abigail, we must pray for people like them. They are not like us, and we must live by example," Sister Mary Margaret reminded her.

Taking the poster upstairs to her bedroom, she re-read it. As much as the thought of Sloane stung her, Sister Mary Margaret was right; she had always been taught about forgiveness and its importance to forgive others. She shouldn't hold a grudge. Sloane and Aisling were in their darkest hour right now, but she had no way of contacting her. It had been over a month since Abigail had sent her that text asking to talk to her, and she never responded. Maybe this was the reason she couldn't answer. She was too caught up with charges ever to face her to speak. No, instead Abigail and Sister Mary Thomas and Sister Mary Margaret would go, but they would go not as supporters. Instead, they would attend with forgiveness in their hearts, witnesses for God.

Chapter Fourteen

ABINGTON SQUARE

The next morning, the townspeople filled the court, as Aisling and Sloane were lead in by handcuffs. Their faces were pale and chalky. Dr. Matthew stood in front of the court. Aisling's face was stone cold. She felt her mother's presence throughout the room. *To trust a human would be a sin. To not trust in human power would be an even bigger sin.* These were words for her and Sloane to hold on to today, as she stared at the townspeople who were mocking her. "Burn the witch!" Yelled a young man in the crowd.

Aisling and Sloane stood in front of the court, their hands chained together. Miles announced the defendants, Aisling Turnberry, and Sloane Turnberry charged with committing acts of witchcraft. He announced to the townspeople that Mavis Edwards would represent the Town of Abington Square. Kelsey Moore would represent Aisling Turnberry and Sloane Turnberry.

Mavis Edwards called Aisling to the stand, as she was sworn in. "You are hereby charged with of not having a fear of God in you, but instead, you are in partnership with Satan the grand enemy of God and man, and that by his instigation and help you are instead in a preternatural way afflicted and done harm to the people who were sick in Abington Square. By the law of God and the Town of Abington Square, you deserve to die by hanging. Aisling heard the complaint against her.

"Is it true that you are a witch?" Mavis asked Aisling, as she glanced over at Miles.

"I am not the witch that you make me out to be, I'm one that wants to do good. My daughter and I are not bad. We don't follow in the ways of the Devil. My mother Sara raised us; she was a woman who had a great commitment to protecting us from the judgment of humans," Aisling admitted to Mavis.

Mavis Edwards couldn't believe what he was hearing. Aisling was defending her actions as a good witch. The townspeople sat in the courtroom, as silence filled the room. Turning his attention to Sloane, he asked the same question.

"You have been accused of not having a fear of God in you, but instead, you are in partnership with Satan the grand enemy of God and man, and that by his instigation and help you are instead in a preternatural way afflicted and done harm to the people who were sick in Abington Square. By the law of God and the Town of Abington Square, you deserve to die by hanging. Aisling heard the complaint against her.

"Is it true that you are a witch?"

Sloane looked at the eyes that were staring at her. She could see Abigail and the nuns sitting in the back of the room.

"I am a witch."

The jury's eyes grew wide with anger. I faithfully hold to the teachings of witchcraft, the same teachings my grandmother had taught me. I will not be made to feel bad for who I am, and I make no excuses for the good that my mother and I did during our time here in Abington Square."

"We have found witches, might we hang them?" Said the townspeople.

"Hang them!" yelled the crowd.

Mavis Edwards looked at the two women sitting before him, one was giving a confession, and the other was vague with her answers. He felt that they were both witches, who refused to take responsibility for their actions.

"What lead you here to Abington Square?" Aisling knew the true answer to that question. It was so Sloane would know Miles and build some communication between them. That had failed. He did just as she thought he would; his faith was greater, so she lied.

"We came here looking for a new life." It wasn't entirely untrue. She was looking to start over and work as a nurse. She wasn't given many chances to help others. As soon as she began to heal people with the oils, honey, and mixtures; she immediately held with suspicion. No one wanted someone who used treatment alternatives. People felt safer using medicines that caused them to feel sicker, even if it meant that they wouldn't heal.

Mavis Edwards wanted to reveal just what these mixtures were and why they were so important to their healing. He tried to think of the right question, but all that could come out was what the mixtures were exactly.

"How did you come to make these mixtures?" he asked Aisling.

"They were made of the finest ingredients taught by my mother. They have healing abilities." Sloane quickly chimed in.

"They are from my mother's recipes," Aisling answered. "They are in a book that my grandmother had given to me before she passed away," Sloane confirmed.

"No more questions," Mavis Edwards looked at the two defendants, as he told the court before sitting down before Kelsey Moore stood up to face the defendants.

Truth is, the evidence was hard to refute. Sloane had already admitted to witchcraft and Aisling had given a vague answer. It would be difficult to show their innocence. Maybe they didn't care about being innocent. They didn't seem to be trying to hide anything. Let's face it; today could be their breath of fresh air. As he approached Aisling and Sloane, he only had one question for them.

"What is in the book?" Kelsey Moore knew it was the wrong question to ask, but Aisling and Sloane weren't helping their case. Taking a short pause, Sloane looked at Aisling before answering.

"It has recipes in it." Her answer was vague. The townspeople turned to each other in small conversations that began to overpower the interior of the courtroom.

"Order...order!" yelled Dr. Matthew.

The crowd's conversations began to stop slowly. Many had a suspicion that recipes meant spells, evil spells. Kelsey Moore walked away from the defendants, *"No further questions."* Taking a seat, he felt helpless. He couldn't think of anything else to say.

"Please give your closing arguments, Mr. Edwards," directed Dr. Matthew.

"Members of the jury. You have overwhelming evidence that these women, Aisling Turnberry, and Sloane Turnberry, is indeed a witch. You have the testimony of their use of oils, honey, and mixtures, a cover-up to use these ingredients to produce evil and to the people that they treated here in Abington Square," Mr. Edwards looked around the room.

"You have heard that not only have they allowed the Devil to enter our community, but their long history of evil through their grandmother and mother. What other possible explanation is there than witchcraft?" His face began to perspire.

"Again, what other reasonable explanation is there for that obvious sign from the Devil? Help rid Abington Square of these horrible creatures before more of our people are stricken. Find Aisling Turnberry and Sloane Turnberry guilty of witchcraft!" Mr. Edwards shouted.

Kelsey Moore stood up in front of the people.

"Members of the jury: What has happened to this community? We have a couple of women who have been caught healing people from sickness. Nurses didn't do anything to harm their patients. They used healing ingredients and hid them so as not to be accused of any crimes. Why? Because it is all a big act," he looked at the jury's stark faces.

"The grandmother and mother's book of recipes. What proof do we have of it? You could see how fake that was, couldn't you? That is what the prosecutor calls evidence. I call it a big joke. If you use honey, then you must be a witch!" Kelsey emphasized.

"Members of the jury, we moved to this town to get away from the harsh treatment of the surrounding cities and towns, just as Aisling and Sloane had done. We moved here so that we could practice our religions freely, and we could have our system of justice," Kelsey took in a deep breath.

"The only justice, in this case, would be to find my clients, Aisling Turnberry and Sloane Turnberry, not guilty of this crime." Taking a seat, Kelsey Moore watched the expressions of the jury.

ABIGAIL

Abigail sat with Sister Mary Thomas and Sister Mary Margaret for the entire day of testimony. She never knew that Sloane had a book of recipes given to her by her grandmother. Although she was pretty sure they weren't the same recipes like the ones that she had used to cook the nun's meals. No, they would be much more complicated than that, maybe sayings and words to use to help to heal those who were sick. Abigail feared for Sloane and Aisling. They may have been witches, but they never tried to force their thinking on her. They seemed to be like any other person. She and Sister Mary Thomas and Sister Mary Margaret waited for a decision of the Jury.

ABINGTON SQUARE

It took less than an hour to return a verdict. The townspeople sat in the courtroom, waiting for justice to be determined. Dr. Matthew turned his attention to the jury. *"Do we have a decision?"* The foreman, a strikingly younger gentleman in his early forties. Those who had sat on the jury were mostly retired men and women, who moved to Abington Square to get away from the politics of a formal justice system. They wanted better control over what happened over the town, and so they turned to Abington Square.

Aisling and Sloane didn't seem to move the entire time that they stood trial. Standing to hear their fate, Miles watched their blank expressions. He had lost them. There was no need for apologies for anything that he may have done wrong before becoming a priest. That part of his life was over. Miles and the people of the court waited to hear the verdict. *"We the jury find Aisling Turnberry and Sloane Turnberry guilty of witchcraft!"* The sounds of the townspeople were those of relief and praise. Aisling and Sloane didn't make a sound. Dr. Matthew addressed the people. "We should not look at today as a day of victory, but one of justice." As the watchmen walked toward Aisling and Sloane, their hands still chained together they walked the distance through town to the place that they would find eternal rest four days after their judgment.

Chapter Fifteen

AISLING

Her time had finally arrived. She and Sloane took the long walk to Abington Square Fields where they would hang for witchcraft. They briefly looked at one another as they entered the towering black gate where a rope hung around each of their necks. Their hands unchained, Sloane took Aisling's hand and held it. They could see the townspeople waiting with anticipation of their deaths. Looking through the crowd, Aisling looked to see Miles. She couldn't see him in the crowd. She wished at that moment that she could take away the teachings and spells that her mother had given her.

SLOANE

The time had come to say goodbye. She said what was right in the court, even if her mother wouldn't entirely admit at first that they were witches. But they didn't make oils and potions; they did more than that, they healed what their town physician couldn't do. She would make no apologies for her behavior. Well— maybe one. She should have answered Abigail when she texts her. It was too late for that now. She had to come to peace with the fact of knowing that she and Aisling would be joined with her grandmother again. Deep down inside, she remembered visiting the nuns and listening to their prayers. She wished that she could be like them, but she wouldn't share that thinking with her mother. Although she wished she did. Partnering with the Devil? She hadn't done such a thing. She despised the work of evil. It was the reason why she and her mother only used honey and all-natural oils. Those were their potions. She didn't bring torrential rain. She didn't have that kind of power. It was just by luck that the weather had changed. Why didn't anyone understand that they weren't witches? It was all fake, just like Kelsey Moore had told the jury.

ABIGAIL

Sorrow filled Abigail's heart as she watched Aisling and Sloane with their necks held by a thin piece of rope. The tall oak tree held the fate of her friend and her mother. She had never seen a person get hung before. The last time this had happened was years before she was even born. Abigail stood in the front amongst all the townspeople. She looked over at Sloane and mouthed the words *"I'm sorry."* Sloane gave a slight mouthing of the words *"Me too"* back to Abigail.

 Watching her best friend hang by a rope was too much to bear. Abigail's heart began to sink. Miles had left to return to Paige Chapel. She thought about leaving too. She had made what she could right with Sloane. She felt it was wrong to watch her friend go through such torture.

ABINGTON SQUARE

Dr. Matthew pulled hard on the long rope. Aisling could hear the words of her mother Sara, *"to trust a human would be a sin. To trust in human power would be an even bigger sin."* She was right. She shouldn't have ever trusted in the people of Abington Square, but it was too late now. She would find comfort in knowing that she would join her mother again.

 "Stop!" yelled Miles. The townspeople were taken back by him.

"We must learn to forgive and to give forgiveness. I can't let you do this to them." His heart stung with intense pain. Miles turned to Aisling and Sloane.

"There is forgiveness and the power of God. There was forgiveness for all, and there was salvation for all who believed," Miles told them.

"Do you believe this?" Miles asked.

"We do believe and we do fear God. I've never fully accepted witchcraft. I never told you my feelings, Sloane. Grandmother forced me to live by witchcraft," Aisling confessed.

She gazed deeply into Miles's eyes. It was undeniable that they still had feelings for each other.

"The more that I saw you, Father Miles, the more I wanted to serve the same God that you do," she whispered under breath.

Maybe it was out of fear, but the feelings to turn away from Sara's teachings had been a long time coming for Aisling. Sloane's face began to tear.

"I wanted to help more. I spent so much with Abigail and the nuns," Sloane confessed.

She hadn't started talking about witchcraft or Sara's book until she had a falling out with Abigail. She was hurt by her best friend. Sloane didn't know how to express her feelings too well. She mostly hid away and shut people out. That was how Aisling taught her. She didn't lead by example for her daughter.

"Do you believe?" he whispered to them.

"Yes, Father Miles, we do," they said in unison.

"Sloane and I know that the people of Abington Square are afraid of us, but know that we do believe," Aisling told him.

"Then if you truly believe with your heart, repeat these words after me." Taking out a prayer from his Bible, Miles gave these words:

"Lord Jesus, I ask you to forgive my sins and save me from eternal separation from God. By faith, I accept Your work and death on the cross as sufficient payment for my sins. Thank You for providing the way for me to know you and to have a relationship with my heavenly Father. Through faith in You, I have eternal life. In Jesus' name, amen," Miles closed in prayer.

"Should we continue with the handing?" asked Dr. Matthew. "We shouldn't hang them," he told the townspeople.

"Let them die!" Yelled the people.

"They are saved. They are children of God. They're now new creatures in Him!" Miles told them. Dr. Matthew stepped away from the rope.

"I can't do this. Untie them!" he demanded the watchmen.

With all their might they tied to get the rope off of them, but it was too late. The rope had become tangled into knots. Sloane felt the tightness of the rope around her neck. Chocking off her air supply, she took her last breath. *"Someone, do something!"* Yelled Sister Mary Thomas. Their air supply is becoming less and less!"

The people watched as the bodies of Aisling and Sloane Turnberry hung lifeless from the lush oak tree. Checking their pulse, Dr. Matthew declared them to be dead.

"It's over and done!" the townspeople cheered in celebration, as an older man took out light and lit the hay that was next to an old oak tree just as Miles had left the old oak tree.

"Burn them!" he yelled.

"We don't believe that their profession of faith was true," yelled the townspeople.

Abigail's heart rushed with pain. *"No--don't!"* she yelled. She ran toward Sloane who was hanging near a stack of hay. She could hear her best friend's words. *Remember, you swore not to tell a soul. We are soul sisters."*

"Abigail! Don't move! Come back!" yelled Sister Mary Thomas and Sister Mary Margaret.

Abigail got close to where Sloane was hanging. The fire from the haystack became bigger and bigger before engulfing Abigail into the fiery flames. The townspeople were in horror. Abigail was gone. Sister Mary Thomas and Sister Mary Margaret cried for their loss.

*****

A few days later, and without a body to bury, Sister Mary Thomas and Sister Mary Margaret held a small ceremony in Paige Chapel for Abigail. Miles gave a sermon on the Book of Daniel on the judgment. It may not have been the sermon he would have given initially, but he felt that the townspeople needed to hear it.

"Out of sight, out of mind. I try to use that little trick at home. If candy is sitting out in a dish in the kitchen, I'm probably going to eat some as I pass by; if it's in the cabinet, it's far more likely to stay there. Sometimes, though, do we treat Judgment Day like the candy that's in the cabinet, something that is there, but maybe we try to forget that it's there, that it's coming?" Miles spoke solemnly.

"In Daniel's vision this morning, the reality of Judgment Day is unavoidable, and perhaps in the vivid picture language that God employs to us about this day may be a bit scary. However, Jesus assured us in the Gospel, we do not need to fear, because judgment is seated in the ancient days, and this is what is seen in the Book of Daniel, but you see do so we have the confidence in the verdict," Miles took a deep breath.

"It's easy to start to wonder if God meant what he promised about bringing his people back home. It's easy to think that maybe he had forgotten about them, or maybe he was just a fable and old wives' tale in the end that had no basis in reality. Daniel's visions are, in part, a reminder that not only is God real, not only is God powerful, but everything that he's said is going to come to pass, even Judgment Day.

"And yet this is the God whom we will stand before in judgment. There's no avoiding it. Daniel's clear in his accounting here: the court sat in judgment, and the books will be opened. There is going to be judgment taking place here. When the Ancient of Days speaks, you listen; when he judges, there's no going back on that judgment. There are no appeals in God's court; all decisions are final," his voice spoke with anger.

"And the nauseating thing about what the conscience says is that it's right. God promised Adam and Eve in the Garden of Eden that if they ate fruit from the forbidden tree, they would certainly die. And this fiery judge with his flaming judgment, this is the death that God had in mind. Not a peaceful heart attack in sleep; not a long, painful fight with cancer. No, eternal death, everlasting suffering in the fires of hell. To sin against the eternal God brings eternal punishment on that sinner. And that's every one of us.

And so what do you say? What could you possibly do to change any of this? There's not enough water in the universe to extinguish a flame-like that. There's no way to change our status. We're guilty, and there's no plea bargain, there's no way to bring the charges down to a misdemeanor. In this court, either you're perfect, or you're not, and if you're not, it means capital punishment," Miles felt his heart pound with pain, as he tried to hold back the tears that he felt for losing Aisling and Sloane.

Miles led Sister Mary Thomas, Sister Mary Margaret, and all the townspeople into the rose garden behind Paige Chapel. It was there that they had sung a familiar hymn before planting a new lavender rose bush in Abigail's memory. She always loved the smell of the garden's roses before preparing dinner. Abigail would walk through the rows of delicate, soft rose petals that gave beauty to the living quarters.

"Jesus. Jesus. Jesus.

There is something about that name.

Master. Savior. Jesus.
Like the fragrance after the rain.
Jesus. Jesus. Jesus. Let all heaven and earth proclaim.
That kings and kingdoms will all pass away.
But there is something about that name."

MILES

Miles watched as Sister Mary Thomas and Sister Mary Margaret had a headstone placed in Abington Square Cemetery with the words inscribed on it: *Well Done, Thou Good and Faithful Servant.* Every week they visited Abigail's grave to leave her flowers and to pray. Next to her grave, Miles knelt down and placed a bouquet of Gerber Daisies for Sloane and a second bouquet of lavender roses for Aisling.

"She was always cheerful and could make Abigail smile," Sister Mary Thomas told Miles.

"Yes, they were good for each other," Miles wiped away his tears.

"Reverend Miles, if I may ask, why the lavender roses for Aisling?"

"It's complicated, Sister Mary Thomas. "I wish that I could explain. But lavender roses are the flower of love."

"You can tell us anything," confirmed Sister Mary Margaret.

"All that I can say is that Aisling was an important person to me, and Sloane was just as important," Miles told them as he stood up.

"Good friends are hard to come by," said Sister Mary Thomas.

"Yes, good friends are a gift from God," Miles answered, "Just like Abigail was to Sloane."

"So young and talented, she wouldn't ever be able to open that restaurant or soup kitchen that she had dreamed about doing in life," Sister Mary Thomas told Miles.

"She is celebrating with the angels in heaven," Miles put his hand on her shoulder and tried to comfort her.

"I know, but the covenant isn't the same without her," Sister Mary Thomas confessed, as the tears began to roll down her cheeks.

"It feels like I did her funeral yesterday, when really it's been almost a month. There is certainly a void here in Abington Square without her," Miles told her. "This could have all been avoided."

"What do you mean?" Sister Mary Thomas asked, "How?"

"Do you remember when you were sick?" asked Miles.

"Yes, Aisling did something to heal me," said Sister Mary Thomas.

"She was a special person," Miles spoke in a soft voice, "They should have been given the chance to live."

"I agree, we shouldn't judge each other," Sister Mary Thomas took a deep breathe. She watched as Miles walked back into Paige Chapel.

*****

Miles took out an old photo of Aisling and Sloane when she was first born. He felt such great mourning overpower him, as he spent most of his time now in his study. Paige Chapel wasn't the same for him. He came to Abington Square to find hope, but after Aisling and Sloane had been hung, he found it difficult to not think about the harshness of the people.

It had been three weeks since Miles had visited the old oak tree where Aisling and Sloane were hung. Their bodies, like Abigail's, were engulfed in flames. He would never forget them. He decided that he would live his life alone. It was the least that he could do after losing them, especially Aisling.

Opening his Bible, he came to Psalm 51, a prayer for forgiveness. He wouldn't judge them, but he felt everyone, including himself, should find forgiveness.

"Be merciful to me, O God, because of your constant love. Because of your great mercy wipe away my sins! Wash away all my evil and make me clean from my sin! I recognize my faults; I am always conscious of my sins. I have sinned against you—only against you—and do what you consider evil," Miles closed the Bible that he had used so many times during his career as a priest.

Miles knew that it was time to move on and see other parts of the country. Maybe he would settle in a bigger town, maybe even a city there would be lots of opportunities to help those who less fortunate. That's what he would do.

Opening his dresser drawers, he took out his clothes one by one and placed them into a brown leather suitcase. He placed his teachings, books, and Bible into a box and carried them down the two blocks to Abington Square Train Station. He could see the gothic top of Paige Chapel, as the roar of the train pulled up. Without looking back, he knew that his time in Abington Square was over. After the hangings of Aisling and Sloane, Miles saw how judgmental the townspeople could be. He witnessed some change such as Dr. Matthew stepping down from being Town Keeper. The pressure alone was too much for him, and he learned the focus would be placed instead on what he cared about the most, which were his patients.

The train glided silently into the station that cast a shadow over the platform and the crowd of passengers who waited nearby. Miles had never felt so alone. Walking toward the train's open doors, a rush of people quickly filtered in as the cool dampness of rain began to fall hard. Taking a seat near the window, Miles stared out the window to take one last look at Abington Square.

"All aboard!" a final call was given to passengers.

"Waaank— Waaank!"

The sound of the train horn signaled the end of a chapter for Miles. The roar of the engine rung loudly as it slowly moved away further and further away from Abington Square. He didn't know what the future held for him. Some may have said that he was taking a train to nowhere. For the first time, Miles had no direction, no plan for what the future would hold. He was okay with that, as long as he was able to keep the A Time to Escape to himself, and the love for that girl he had met on that cool November morning. He would never forget Aisling and the love that they shared. It was his secret, and he would keep it protected, deep within his heart forever.

AISLING

Bong! Bong! The loud noise rang from the steeple of the old gothic church. A young woman with long flowing ginger hair sat quietly in the first pew of Seeth Church. Her eyelids closed tightly, the loud noise pierced her. Opening her eyes, she looked around the rugged interior of dark wood that was fashioned by décor of the rows of pews that were behind her. The large rusty iron pipes from the organ stood solemnly against the wall. She continued to look around the church as if it were the first time that she had been inside.

"I don't understand what has happened?" she thought to herself. Getting up from the front pew, she swiftly walked down the center aisle. Her heart began to pump harder and harder, as if she may collapse or have a heart attack.

Bong! Bong! The ringing of the bells became even louder as she approached the front doors. The bright sunlight glowed and gave shine to the open fields surrounding Seeth Chapel. She could feel the warmth of the sun, as it felt warm on her body. The young woman opened the heavy wooden doors to the chapel.

"Excuse me," a deep voice startled her. She hadn't even noticed the tall, chestnut colored-haired man that was walking up the front steps of the church.

"I'm Miles," introducing himself, he carried a bouquet of lavender roses.

"Aisling," she said. She stared for what felt like an hour, as the memories of Abington Square flooded her thinking.

"Was it all a dream? Or am I seeing into my future?" The book of spells flew open, a rumble of thunder and the howling echo of the wind filled Seeth Chapel, as she could hear the words of her grandmother's spell. *"To trust a human would be a sin. To trust in human power would be an even bigger sin."*

QUESTIONS AND TOPICS FOR DISCUSSION

1. Why do you think Sara had so much anger towards humans? What are her hesitations and fears? Do you agree with her decision to keep Aisling away from humans?

2. Throughout this novel, Aisling wants nothing more but to like every human. Do you feel that it's possible given her long family history of witchcraft that she could be like and accepted as human? Why does Aisling struggle with herself?

3. Why do you think Aisling agreed to bring Sloane to Abington Square? What challenges might be faced in starting a new life away from Maple Hill? Do you agree with her decision, given their lack of acceptance by the townspeople?

4. Throughout this novel, Miles and Aisling struggle to keep their love for each other neutral. What do you think of Miles's emotions about Aisling and how he handled their bond? What do you think of Aisling's reactions and feelings toward Miles and his mistakes? Why does Aisling struggle to let him go, even though he hasn't revealed to Sloane that he is her father?

5. What role does Miles play in Sloane's life? Do you feel that he should have revealed his identity to her?

6. Miles Dowse had great faith that Aisling and Sloane had left witchcraft. Were there other characters that had the same belief as Miles did in this story?

7. Discuss the role of forgiveness in the book: Which characters are struggling to forgive others or be forgiven themselves?

8. What role does Abington Square have in the novel? How does it provide refuge for the characters, and why is that important to Aisling and Sloane in particular? Discuss how that refuge is interrupted or violated throughout the book?

9. Throughout the novel, there are many attempts to rekindle relationships, from the friendship bond between Abigail and his daughter Sloane to the romantic history between Aisling and her old boyfriend Miles. Which relationships are healed and strengthened by the end of the novel, and in what ways? What new relationships are forged?

10. For Miles, losing almost everything helped give him a perspective on what he truly values and needs in his life. By the end of the novel, what do you think Miles has discovered what's important? Has he been able to regain what matters most to him?

ABOUT THE AUTHOR

Cristina Guarneri has been a writer of books and short stories, for the last eighteen years. In addition to writing, she has been a college professor for the last nine years. Focusing on topics that promote positive thinking, she has developed *A Novel Idea*, an organization dedicated to promoting reading awareness and writing workshops for adults.

Cristina has spoken on national radio for the last two years, speaking in the top 30-radio market. In 2014, Cristina presented her first novel *See No Evil* during BookExpo in New York City, which was written into the play *Trial and Treason*. *Trial and Treason* won the New Jersey's Playwright Contest at William Paterson University, Wayne, NJ. Cristina continued to work on various writing projects, including writing her book *El Shaddai* into her first play and her second play entitled *House of Deception.*

Cristina holds a doctorate from Seton Hall University. She is the author of *See No Evil, The Inceptor's Covenant, El Shaddai, Twitterocracy, and Twitterocracy: Social Media and Democracy, House of Deception, Veil of Secrecy, and Solomon Vow,* along with the children's books *Purple Ribbons, The Magic Tree,* and *Just Being Me.*

I think if I've learned anything about friendship, it's to hang in, stay connected, fight for them, and let them fight for you. Don't walk away; don't be distracted. Don't be too busy or tired. Don't take your friends for granted. Friends are part of the glue that holds life and faith together. Powerful stuff.

—John Katz